Wels

Willia

Jan Webmedia

JAN WEBMEDIA CLASSICS

WORLD FAIRY TALES

English Fairy Tales (Jacobs): paperback, hardcover
Welsh Fairy Tales (Griffis): paperback, hardcover
Scottish Fairy Tales (Grierson): paperback, hardcover
Irish Fairy Tales (Yeats): paperback, hardcover
Manx Fairy Tales (Morrison): paperback, hardcover

And many more from all around the world.

janwebmedia.uk

Welsh

Fairy Tales

William Elliot Griffis

Jan Webmedia

Cambridge

ISBN: 979-8429853543 Paperback
ISBN: 979-8813210365 Hardcover

Published by: Jan Webmedia, Cambridge
Published in May 2022, 1st edition
Book cover design: Jan Webmedia
Formatting: Jan Webmedia

janwebmedia.uk

Contents

A Preface-Letter to my Grandfather

Dear Captain John Griffis

Although I never saw you, since you died in 1804, I am glad you were one of those Welshmen who opposed the policy of King George III and that you, after coming to America in 1783, were among the first sea captains to carry the American flag around the world. That you knew many of the Free Quakers and other patriots of the Revolution and that they buried you among them, near Benjamin Franklin, is a matter of pride to your descendants. That you were born in Wales and spoke Welsh, as did also those three great prophets of spiritual liberty, Roger Williams, William Penn, and Thomas Jefferson, is still further ground for pride in one's ancestry. Now, in the perspective of history we see that our Washington and his compeers and Wilkes, Barre, Burke and the friends of America in Parliament were fighting the same battle of Freedom. Though our debt to Wales for many things is great, we count not least those inheritances from the world of imagination, for which the Cymric Land was famous, even before the days of either Anglo-Saxon or Norman.

William Elliot Griffis
Saint David's and the day of the Daffodil, March 1, 1921

WELSH RABBIT AND HUNTED HARES

Long, long ago, there was a good saint named David, who taught the early Cymric or Welsh people better manners and many good things to eat and ways of enjoying themselves.

Now the Welsh folks in speaking of their good teacher pronounced his name Tafid and affectionately Taffy, and this came to be the usual name for a person born in Wales. In our nurseries we all learned that "Taffy was a Welshman," but it was their enemies who made a bad rhyme about Taffy.

Wherever there were cows or goats, people could get milk. So they always had what was necessary for a good meal, whether it were breakfast, dinner or supper. Milk, cream, curds, whey and cheese enriched the family table. Were not these enough?

But Saint David taught the people how to make a still more delicious food out of cheese, and that this could be done without taking the life of any creature.

Saint David showed the girls how to take cheese, slice and toast it over the coals, or melt it in a skillet and pour it hot over toast or biscuit. This gave the cheese a new and sweeter flavor. When spread on bread, either plain, or browned over the fire, the result, in combination, was a delicacy fit for a king, and equal to anything known.

The fame of this new addition to the British bill of fare spread near and far. The English people, who had always been fond of rabbit pie, and still eat thousands of Molly Cotton Tails every day, named it "Welsh Rabbit," and thought it one of the best things to eat. In fact, there are many people, who do not easily see a joke, who misunderstand the fun, or who suppose the name to be either slang, or vulgar, or a mistake, and who call it "rarebit." It is like "Cape Cod turkey" (codfish), or "Bombay ducks" (dried fish), or "Irish plums" (potatoes) and such funny cookery with fancy names.

Now up to this time, the rabbits and hares had been so hunted with the aid of dogs, that there was hardly a chance of any of them surviving the cruel slaughter.

In the year 604, the Prince of Powys was out hunting. The dogs started a hare, and pursued it into a dense thicket. When the hunter with the horn came up, a strange sight met his eyes. There he saw a lovely maiden. She was kneeling on the ground and devoutly praying. Though surprised at this, the prince was anxious to secure his game. He hissed on the hounds and ordered the horn to be blown, for the dogs to charge on their prey, expecting them to bring him the game at once. Instead of this, though they were trained dogs and would fight even a wolf, they slunk away howling, and frightened, as if in pain, while the horn stuck fast to the lips of the blower and he was silent. Meanwhile, the hare nestled under the maiden's dress and seemed not in the least disturbed.

Amazed at this, the prince turned to the fair lady and asked: "Who are you?"

She answered, "My mother named me Monacella. I have fled from Ireland, where my father wished to marry me to one of his chief men, whom I did not love. Under God's guidance, I came to this secret desert place, where I have lived for fifteen years, without seeing the face of man."

To this, the prince in admiration replied: "O most worthy Melangell [which is the way the Welsh pronounce Monacella], because, on account of thy merits, it has pleased God to shelter and save this little, wild hare, I, on my part, herewith present thee with this land, to be for the service of God and an asylum for all men and women, who seek thy protection. So long as they do not pollute this sanctuary, let none, not even prince or chieftain, drag them forth."

The beautiful saint passed the rest of her life in this place. At night, she slept on the bare rock. Many were the wonders wrought for those who with pure hearts sought her refuge. The little wild hares were under her special protection, and they are still called "Melangell's Lambs."

THE MIGHTY MONSTER AFANG

After the Cymric folk, that is, the people we call Welsh, had come up from Cornwall into their new land, they began to cut down the trees, to build towns, and to have fields and gardens. Soon they made the landscape smile with pleasant homes, rich farms and playing children.

They trained vines and made flowers grow. The young folks made pets of the wild animals' cubs, which their fathers and big brothers brought home from hunting. Old men took rushes and reeds and wove them into cages for song birds to live in.

While they were draining the swamps and bogs, they drove out the monsters, that had made their lair in these wet places. These terrible creatures liked to poison people with their bad breath, and even ate up very little boys and girls, when they strayed away from home.

So all the face of the open country between the forests became very pretty to look at. The whole of Cymric land, which then extended from the northern Grampian Hills to Cornwall, and from the Irish Sea, past their big fort, afterward called London, even to the edge of the German Ocean, became a delightful place to live in.

The lowlands and the rivers, in which the tide rose and fell daily, were especially attractive. This was chiefly because of the many bright flowers growing there; while the yellow gorse and the pink heather made the hills look as lovely as a young girl's face. Besides this, the Cymric maidens were the prettiest ever, and the lads were all brave and healthy; while both of these knew how to sing often and well.

Now there was a great monster named the Afang, that lived in a big bog, hidden among the high hills and inside of a dark, rough forest.

This ugly creature had an iron-clad back and a long tail that could wrap itself around a mountain. It had four front legs, with big knees that were bent up like a grasshopper's, but were covered with scales like armor. These were as hard as steel, and bulged out at the thighs. Along its back, was a ridge of horns, like spines, and higher than an alligator's. Against such a tough hide, when the hunters shot their darts and hurled their javelins, these weapons fell down to the ground, like harmless pins.

On this monster's head, were big ears, half way between those of a jackass and an elephant. Its eyes were as green as leeks, and were round, but scalloped on the edges, like squashes, while they were as big as pumpkins.

The Afang's face was much like a monkey's, or a gorilla's, with long straggling gray hairs around its cheeks like those of a walrus. It always looked as if a napkin, as big as a bath towel, would be necessary to keep its mouth clean. Yet even then, it slobbered a good deal, so that no nice fairy liked to be near the monster.

When the Afang growled, the bushes shook and the oak leaves trembled on the branches, as if a strong wind was blowing.

But after its dinner, when it had swallowed down a man, or two calves, or four sheep, or a fat heifer, or three goats, its body swelled up like a balloon. Then it usually rolled over, lay along the ground, or in the soft mud, and felt very stupid and sleepy, for a long while.

All around its lair, lay wagon loads of bones of the creatures, girls, women, men, boys, cows, and occasionally a donkey, which it had devoured.

But when the Afang was ravenously hungry and could not get these animals and when fat girls and careless boys were scarce, it would live on birds, beasts and fishes. Although it was very fond of cows and sheep, yet the wool and hair of these an - imals stuck in its big teeth, it often felt very miserable and its usually bad temper grew worse.

Then, like a beaver, it would cut down a tree, sharpen it to a point and pick its teeth until its mouth was clean. Yet it seemed all the more hungry and eager for fresh human victims to eat, especially juicy maidens; just as children like cake more than bread.

The Cymric men were not surprised at this, for they knew that girls were very sweet and they almost worshiped women. So they learned to guard their daughters and wives. They saw that to do such things as eating up people was in the nature of the beast, which could never be taught good manners.

But what made them mad beyond measure was the trick which the monster often played upon them by breaking the river banks, and the dykes which with great toil they had built to protect their crops. Then the waters overflowed all their farms, ruined their gardens and spoiled their cow houses and stables.

This sort of mischief the Afang liked to play, especially about the time when the oat and barley crops were ripe and ready to be gathered to make cakes and flummery; that is sour oat-jelly, or pap. So it often happened that the children had to do without their cookies and porridge during the winter. Some - times the floods rose so high as to wash away the houses and float the cradles. Even those with little babies in them were of - ten seen on the raging waters, and sent dancing on the waves down the river, to the sea.

Once in a while, a mother cat and all her kittens were seen mewing for help, or a lady dog howling piteously. Often it happened that both puppies and kittens were drowned.

So, whether for men or mothers, pussies or puppies, the

Cymric men thought the time had come to stop this monster's mischief. It was bad enough that people should be eaten up, but to have all their crops ruined and animals drowned, so that they had to go hungry all winter, with only a little fried fish, and no turnips, was too much for human patience. There were too many weeping mothers and sorrowful fathers, and squalling brats and animals whining for something to eat.

Besides, if all the oats were washed away, how could their wives make flummery, without which, no Cymric man is ever happy? And where would they get seed for another year's sow-ing? And if there were no cows, how could the babies or kitties live, or any grown-up persons get buttermilk?

Someone may ask, why did not some brave man shoot the Afang, with a poisoned arrow, or drive a spear into him under the arms, where the flesh was tender, or cut off his head with a sharp sword?

The trouble was just here. There were plenty of brave fel-lows, ready to fight the monster, but nothing made of iron could pierce that hide of his. This was like armor, or one of the steel battleships of our day, and the Afang always spit out fire or poison breath down the road, up which a man was coming, long before the brave fellow could get near him. Nothing would do, but to go up into his lair, and drag him out.

But what man or company of men was strong enough to do this, when a dozen giants in a gang, with ropes as thick as a ship's hawser, could hardly tackle the job?

Nevertheless, in what neither man nor giant could do, a pretty maiden might succeed. True, she must be brave also, for how could she know, but if hungry, the Afang might eat her up?

However, one valiant damsel, of great beauty, who had lots of perfumery and plenty of pretty clothes, volunteered to bind the monster in his lair. She said, "I'm not afraid." Her sweet-heart was named Gadern, and he was a young and strong hunter. He talked over the matter with her and they two re-solved to act together.

14

Gadern went all over the country, summoning the farmers to bring their ox teams and log chains. Then he set the black-smiths to work, forging new and especially heavy ones, made of the best native iron, from the mines, for which Wales is still famous.

Meanwhile, the lovely maiden arrayed herself in her pretti-est clothes, dressed her hair in the most enticing way, hanging a white blossom on each side, over her ears, with one flower also at her neck.

When she had perfumed her garments, she sallied forth and up the lake where the big bog and the waters were and where the monster hid himself.

While the maiden was still quite a distance away, the terrible Afang, scenting his visitor from afar, came rushing out of his lair. When very near, he reared his head high in the air, expect-ing to pounce on her, with his iron clad claws and at one swallow make a breakfast of the girl.

But the odors of her perfumes were so sweet, that he forgot what he had thought to do. Moreover, when he looked at her, he was so taken with unusual beauty, that he flopped at once on his forefeet. Then he behaved just like a lovelorn beau, when his best girl comes near. He ties his necktie and pulls down his coat and brushes off the collar.

So the Afang began to spruce up. It was real fun to see how a monster behaves when smitten with love for a pretty girl. He had no idea how funny he was.

The girl was not at all afraid, but smoothed the monster's back, stroked and played with its big moustaches and tickled its neck until the Afang's throat actually gurgled with a laugh. Pretty soon he guffawed, for he was so delighted.

When he did this, the people down in the valley thought it was thunder, though the sky was clear and blue.

The maiden tickled his chin, and even put up his whiskers in curl papers. Then she stroked his neck, so that his eyes closed. Soon she had gently lulled him to slumber, by singing a cradle song, which her mother had taught her. This she did so softly, and sweetly, that in a few minutes, with its head in her lap, the monster was sound asleep and even began to snore.

Then, quietly, from their hiding places in the bushes, Gadern and his men crawled out. When near the dreaded Afang, they stood up and sneaked forward, very softly on tip toe. They had wrapped the links of the chain in grass and leaves, so that no clanking was heard. They also held the oxen's yokes, so that nobody or anything could rattle, or make any noise. Slowly but surely they passed the chain over its body, in the middle, besides binding the brute securely between its fore and hind legs.

All this time, the monster slept on, for the girl kept on crooning her melody.

When the forty yoke of oxen were all harnessed together, the drovers cracked all their whips at once, so that it sounded like a clap of thunder and the whole team began to pull together.

Then the Afang woke up with a start.

The sudden jerk roused the monster to wrath, and its bellowing was terrible. It rolled round and round, and dug its four sets of toes, each with three claws, every one as big as a plowshare, into the ground. It tried hard to crawl into its lair, or slip into the lake.

Finding that neither was possible, the Afang looked about, for some big tree to wrap its tail around. But all his writhings or plungings were of no use. The drovers plied their whips and the oxen kept on with one long pull together and forward. They strained so hard, that one of them dropped its eye out. This formed a pool, and to this day they call it The Pool of the Ox's Eye. It never dries up or overflows, though the water in it rises and falls, as regularly as the tides.

For miles over the mountains the sturdy oxen hauled the monster. The pass over which they toiled and strained so hard is still named the Pass of the Oxen's Slope. When going down hill, the work of dragging the Afang was easier.

In a great hole in the ground, big enough to be a pond, they dumped the carcass of the Afang, and soon a little lake was formed. This uncanny bit of water is called "The Lake of the Green Well." It is considered dangerous for man or beast to go too near it. Birds do not like to fly over the surface, and when sheep tumble in, they sink to the bottom at once.

If the bones of the Afang still lie at the bottom, they must have sunk down very deep, for the monster had no more power to get out, or to break the river banks. The farmers no longer cared anything about the creature, and they hardly every think of the old story, except when a sheep is lost.

As for Gadern and his brave and lovely sweetheart, they were married and lived long and happily. Their descendants, in the thirty-seventh generation, are proud of the grand exploit of their ancestors, while all the farmers honor his memory and bless the name of the lovely girl that put the monster asleep.

3

THE TWO CAT WITCHES

In old days, it was believed that the seventh son, in a family of sons, was a conjurer by nature. That is, he could work wonders like the fairies and excel the doctors in curing diseases.

If he were the seventh son of a seventh son, he was himself a wonder of wonders. The story ran that he could even cure the "shingles," which is a very troublesome disease. It is called also by a Latin name, which means a snake, because, as it gets worse, it coils itself around the body.

Now the eagle can attack the serpent and conquer and kill this poisonous creature. To secure such power, Hugh, the conjurer, ate the flesh of eagles. When he wished to cure the serpent-disease, he uttered words in the form of a charm which acted as a talisman and cure. After wetting the red rash, which had broken out over the sick person's body, he muttered:

"He-eagle, she-eagle, I send you over nine seas, and over nine mountains, and over nine acres of moor and fen, where no dog shall bark, no cow low, and no eagle shall higher rise."

After that, the patient was sure that he felt better.

There was always great rivalry between these conjurers and those who made money from the Pilgrims at Holy Wells and visitors to the relic shrines, but this fellow, named Hugh, and the monks, kept on mutually good terms. They often ate dinner together, for Hugh was a great traveler over the whole country and always had news to tell to the holy brothers who lived in cells.

One night, as he was eating supper at an inn, four men came in and sat down at the table with him. By his magical power, Hugh knew that they were robbers and meant to kill him that night, in order to get his money.

So, to divert their attention, Hugh made something like a horn to grow up out of the table, and then laid a spell on the robbers, so that they were kept gazing at the curious thing all night long, while he went to bed and slept soundly.

When he rose in the morning, he paid his bill and went away, while the robbers were still gazing at the horn. Only when the officers arrived to take them to prison did they come to themselves.

Now at Bettws-y-Coed-that pretty place which has a name that sounds so funny to us Americans and suggests a girl named Betty the Co-ed at college—there was a hotel, named the "Inn of Three Kegs." The shop sign hung out in front. It was a bunch of grapes gilded and set below three small barrels.

This inn was kept by two respectable ladies, who were sisters.

Yet in that very hotel, several travelers, while they were asleep, had been robbed of their money. They could not blame anyone nor tell how the mischief was done. With the key in the keyhole, they had kept their doors locked during the night. They were sure that no one had entered the room. There were no signs of men's boots, or of anyone's footsteps in the garden, while nothing was visible on the lock or door, to show that either had been tampered with. Everything was in order as when they went to bed.

Some people doubted their stories, but when they applied to Hugh the conjurer, he believed them and volunteered to solve the mystery. His motto was "Go anywhere and everywhere, but catch the thief."

When Hugh applied one night for lodging at the inn, nothing could be more agreeable than the welcome, and fine manners of his two hostesses.

At supper time, and during the evening, they all chatted together merrily. Hugh, who was never at a loss for news or stories, told about the various kinds of people and the many countries he had visited, in imagination, just as if he had seen them all, though he had never set foot outside of Wales.

When he was ready to go to bed, he said to the ladies:

"It is my custom to keep a light burning in my room, all night, but I will not ask for candles, for I have enough to last me until sunrise." So saying, he bade them good night.

Entering his room and locking the door, he undressed, but laid his clothes near at hand. He drew his trusty sword out of its sheath and laid it upon the bed beside him, where he could quickly grasp it. Then he pretended to be asleep and even snored.

It was not long before, peeping between his eyelids, only half closed, he saw two cats come stealthily down the chimney.

When in the room, the animals frisked about, and then gamboled and romped in the most lively way. Then they chased each other around the bed, as if they were trying to find out whether Hugh was asleep.

Meanwhile, the supposed sleeper kept perfectly motionless. Soon the two cats came over to his clothes and one of them put her paw into the pocket that contained his purse.

At this, with one sweep of his sword, Hugh struck at the cat's paw. The beast howled frightfully, and both animals ran for the chimney and disappeared. After that, everything was quiet until breakfast time.

At the table, only one of the sisters was present. Hugh politely inquired after the other one. He was told that she was not well, for which Hugh said he was very sorry.

After the meal, Hugh declared he must say good-by to both the sisters, whose company he had so enjoyed the night before. In spite of the other lady's many excuses, he was admitted to the sick lady's room.

After polite greetings and mutual compliments, Hugh

offered his hand to say "good-by." The sick lady smiled at once and put out her hand, but it was her left one.

"Oh, no," said Hugh, with a laugh. "I never in all my life have taken any one's left hand, and, beautiful as yours is, I won't break my habit by beginning now and here."

Reluctantly, and as if in pain, the sick lady put out her hand. It was bandaged.

The mystery was now cleared up. The two sisters were cats.

By the help of bad fairies they had changed their forms and were the real robbers.

Hugh seized the hand of the other sister and made a little cut in it, from which a few drops of blood flowed, but the spell was over.

"Henceforth," said Hugh, "you are both harmless, and I trust you will both be honest women."

And they were. From that day they were like other women, and kept one of the best of those inns—clean, tidy, comfortable and at modest prices—for which Wales is, or was, noted.

Neither as cats with paws, nor landladies, with soaring bills, did they ever rob travellers again.

4

How the Cymry Land Became Inhabited

I n all Britain to-day, no wolf roams wild and the deer are all tame.

Yet in the early ages, when human beings had not yet come into the land, the swamps and forests were full of very savage animals. There were bears and wolves by the thousand besides lions and the woolly rhinoceros, tigers, with terrible teeth like sabres.

Beavers built their dams over the little rivers, and the great horned oxen were very common. Then the mountains were higher, and the woods denser. Many of the animals lived in caves, and there were billions of bees and a great many butter-flies. In the bogs were ferns of giant size, amid which terrible monsters hid that were always ready for a fight or a frolic.

In so beautiful a land, it seemed a pity that there were no men and women, no boys or girls, and no babies.

Yet the noble race of the Cymry, whom we call the Welsh, were already in Europe and lived in the summer land in the South. A great benefactor was born among them, who grew up to be a wonderfully wise man and taught his people the use of bows and arrows. He made laws, by which the different tribes stopped their continual fighting and quarrels, and united for the common good of all. He persuaded them to take family names. He invented the plow, and showed them how to use it, making furrows, in which to plant grain.

When the people found that they could get things to eat right out of the ground, from the seed they had planted, their children were wild with joy.

No people ever loved babies more than these Cymry folk and it was they who invented the cradle. This saved the hard-working mothers many a burden, for each woman had, besides rearing the children, to work for and wait on her husband.

He was the warrior and hunter, and she did most of the labor, in both the house and the field. When there were many little brats to look after, a cradle was a real help to her. In those days, "brat" was the general name for little folks. There were good laws, about women especially for their protection. Any rough or brutish fellow was fined heavily, or publicly punished, for striking one of them.

By and by, this great benefactor encouraged his people to the brave adventure, and led them, in crossing the sea to Britain. Men had not yet learned to build boats, with prow or stern, with keels and masts, or with sails, rudders, or oars, or much less to put engines in their bowels, or iron chimneys for smoke stacks, by which we see the mighty ships driven across the ocean without regard to wind or tide.

This great benefactor taught his people to make coracles, and on these the whole tribe of thousands of Cymric folk crossed over into Britain, landing in Cornwall. The old name of this shire meant the Horn of Gallia, or Wallia, as the new land was later named. We think of Cornwall as the big toe of the Mother Land. These first comers called it a horn.

It was a funny sight to see these coracles, which they named after their own round bodies. The men went down to the river-side or the sea shore, and with their stone hatchets, they chopped down trees. They cut the reeds and osiers, peeled the willow branches, and wove great baskets shaped like bowls. In this work, the women helped the men.

The coracle was made strong by a wooden frame fixed inside

round the edge, and by two cross boards, which also served as seats. Then they turned the wicker frame upside down and stretched the hides of animals over the whole frame and bottom. With pitch, gum, or grease, they covered up the cracks or seams. Then they shaped paddles out of wood. When the coracle floated on the water, the whole family, daddy, mammy, kiddies, and any old aunts or uncles, or granddaddies, got into it. They waited for the wind to blow from the south over to the northern land.

At first the coracle spun round and round, but by and by each daddy could, by rowing or paddling, make the thing go straight ahead. So finally all arrived in the land now called Great Britain.

Though sugar was not then known, or for a thousand years later, the first thing they noticed was the enormous number of bees. When they searched, they found the rock caves and hollow trees full of honey, which had accumulated for generations. Every once in a while the bears, that so like sweet things, found out the hiding place of the bees, and ate up the honey. The children were very happy in sucking the honey comb and the mothers made candles out of the beeswax. The new comers named the country Honey Island.

The brave Cymry men had battles with the darker skinned people who were already there. When any one, young or old, died, their friends and relatives sat up all night guarding the body against wild beasts or savage men. This grew to be a settled custom and such a meeting was called a "wake." Everyone present did keep awake, and often in a very lively way.

As the Cymry multiplied, they built many *don*, or towns. All over the land to-day are names ending in *don* like London, or Croydon, showing where these villages were.

But while occupied in things for the body, their great ruler did not neglect matters of the mind. He found that some of his people had good voices and loved to sing. Others delighted in making poetry. So he invented or improved the harp, and fixed the rules of verse and song.

Thus ages before writing was known, the Cymry preserved their history and handed down what the wise ones taught.

Men might be born, live and die, come and go, like leaves on the trees, which expand in the springtime and fall in the autumn; but their songs, and poetry, and noble language never die. Even to-day, the Cymry love the speech of their fathers almost as well as they love their native land.

Yet things were not always lovely in Honey Land, or as sweet as sugar. As the tribes scattered far apart to settle in this or that valley, some had fish, but no salt, and others had plenty of salt, but no fish. Some had all the venison and bear meat they wanted, but no barley or oats. The hill men needed what the men on the seashore could supply. From their sheep and oxen they got wool and leather, and from the wild beasts fur to keep warm in winter. So many of them grew expert in trade. Soon there were among them some very rich men who were the chiefs of the tribes.

In time, hundreds of others learned how to traffic among the tribes and swap, or barter their goods, for as yet there were no coins for money, or bank bills. So they established markets or fairs, to which the girls and boys liked to go and sell their eggs and chickens, for when the wolves and foxes were killed off, sheep and geese multiplied.

But what hindered the peace of the land, were the feuds, or quarrels, because the men of one tribe thought they were braver, or better looking, than those in the other tribe. The women were very apt to boast that they wore their clothes—which were made of fox and weasel skins—more gracefully than those in the tribe next to them.

So there was much snarling and quarreling in Cymric Land. The people were too much like naughty children, or when kiddies are not taught good manners, to speak gently and to be kind one to the other.

One of the worst quarrels broke out, because in one tribe

there were too many maidens and not enough young men for husbands. This was bad for the men, for it spoiled them. They had too many women to wait on them and they grew to be very selfish.

In what might be the next tribe, the trouble was the other way. There were too many boys, a surplus of men, and not nearly enough girls to go round. When any young fellow, moping out his life alone and anxious for a wife, went a-courting in the next tribe, or in their vale, or on their hill top, he was usually driven off with stones. Then there was a quarrel between the two tribes.

Any young girl, who sneaked out at night to meet her young man of another clan, was, when caught, instantly and severely spanked. Then, with her best clothes taken off, she had to stand tied to a post in the market place a whole day. Her hair was pulled down in disorder, and all the dogs were allowed to bark at her. The girls made fun of the poor thing, while they all rubbed one forefinger over the other, pointed at her and cried, "Fie, for shame!" while the boys called her hard names.

If it were known that the young man who wanted a wife had visited a girl in the other tribe, his spear and bow and arrows were taken away from him till the moon was full. The other boys and the girls treated him roughly and called him hard names, but he dare not defend himself and had to suffer patiently. This was all because of the feud between the two tribes.

This went on until the maidens in the valley, who were very many, while yet lovely and attractive, became very lonely and miserable; while the young men, all splendid hunters and warriors, multiplied in the hill country. They were wretched in mind, because not one could get a wife, for all the maidens in their own tribe were already engaged, or had been mated.

One day news came to the young men on the hill top, that the valley men were all off on a hunting expedition. At once, without waiting a moment, the poor lonely bachelors plucked up courage. Then, armed with ropes and straps, they marched in a body to the village in the valley below. There, they seized each man a girl, not waiting for any maid to comb her hair, or put on a new frock, or pack up her clothes, or carry any thing out of her home, and made off with her, as fast as one pair of legs could move with another pair on top.

At first, this looked like rough treatment—for a lovely girl, thus to be strapped to a brawny big fellow; but after a while, the girls thought it was great fun to be married and each one to have a man to caress, and fondle, and scold, and look for, and boss around; for each wife, inside of her own hut was quite able to rule her husband. Every one of these new wives was delighted to find a man who cared so much for her as to come after her, and risk his life to get her, and each one admired her new, brave husband.

Yet the brides knew too well that their men folks, fathers and brothers, uncles and cousins, would soon come back to attempt their recapture.

And this was just what happened. When a runner brought, to the valley men now far away, the news of the rape of their daughters, the hunters at once ceased chasing the deer and marched quickly back to get the girls and make them come home.

The hill men saw the band of hunters coming after their daughters. They at once took their new wives into a natural rocky fortress, on the top of a precipice, which overlooked the lake.

This stronghold had only one entrance, a sort of gateway of rocks, in front of which was a long steep, narrow path. Here the hill men stood, to resist the attack and hold their prizes.

It was a case of a very few defenders, assaulted by a multitude, and the battle was long and bloody. The hill men scorned to surrender and shot their arrows and hurled their javelins with desperate valor. They battled all day from sunrise until the late afternoon, when shadows began to lengthen. The stars, one by one came out and both parties, after setting sentinels, lay down to rest.

In the morning, again, charge after charge was made. Sword beat against shield and helmet, and clouds of arrows were shot by the archers, who were well posted in favorable situations, on the rocks. Long before noon, the field below was dotted and the narrow pass was choked with dead bodies. In the afternoon, after a short rest and refreshed with food, the valley men, though finding that only four of the hill fighters were alive, stood off at a distance and with their long bows and a shower of arrows left not one to breathe.

Now, thought the victors, we shall get our maidens back again. So, taking their time to wash off the blood and dust, to bind up their wounds, and to eat their supper, they thought it would be an easy job to load up all the girls on their ox-carts and carry them home.

But the valley brides, thus suddenly made widows, were too true to their brave husbands. So, when they had seen the last of their lovers quiet in death, they stripped off all their ornaments and fur robes, until all stood together, each clad in her own in-nocence, as pure in their purpose as if they were a company of Druid priestesses.

Then, chanting their death song, they marched in proces-sion to the tall cliff, that rose sheer out of the water. One by one, each uttering the name of her beloved, leaped into the waves.

Men at a distance, knowing nothing of the fight, and sailors and fishermen far off on the water, thought that a flock of white birds were swooping down from their eyrie, into the sea to get their food from the fishes. But when none rose up above the waters, they understood, and later heard the whole story of the valor of the men and the devotion of the women.

The solemn silence of night soon brooded over the scene.

The men of the valley stayed only long enough to bury their own dead. Then they marched home and their houses were filled with mourning. Yet they admired the noble sacrifice of their daughters and were proud of them. Afterwards they raised stone monuments on the field of slaughter.

To-day, this water is called the Lake of the Maidens, and the great stones seen near the beach are the memorials marking the place of the slain in battle.

During many centuries, the ancient custom of capturing the bride, with resistance from her male relatives, was vigorously kept up. In the course of time, however, this was turned into a mimic play, with much fun and merriment. Yet, the girls appear to like it, and some even complain if it is not rough enough to seem almost real.

5

THE BOY THAT WAS NAMED
TROUBLE

In one of the many "Co-eds," or places with this name, in ancient and forest-covered Wales, there was a man who had one of the most beautiful mares in all the world. Yet great misfortunes befell both this Co-ed mare and her owner.

Every night, on the first of May, the mare gave birth to a pretty little colt. Yet no one ever saw, or could ever tell what became of any one, or all of the colts. Each and all, and one by one, they disappeared. Nobody knew where they were, or went, or what had become of them.

At last, the owner, who had no children, and loved little horses, determined not to lose another. He girded on his sword, and with his trusty spear, stood guard all night in the stable to catch the mortal robber, as he supposed he must be.

When on this same night of May first, the mare foaled again, and the colt stood up on its long legs, the man greatly admired the young creature. It looked already, as if it could, with its own legs, run away and escape from any wolf that should chase it, hoping to eat it up.

But at this moment, a great noise was heard outside the stable. The next moment a long arm, with a claw at the end of it, was poked through the window-hole, to seize the colt.

Instantly the man drew his sword and with one blow, the claw part of the arm was cut off, and it dropped inside, with the colt.

Hearing a great cry and tumult outside, the owner of the mare rushed forth into the darkness. But though he heard howls of pain, he could see nothing, so he returned.

There, at the door, he found a baby, with hair as yellow as gold, smiling at him. Besides its swaddling clothes, it was wrapped up in flame-colored satin.

As it was still night, the man took the infant to his bed and laid it alongside of his wife, who was asleep.

Now this good woman loved children, though she had none of her own, and so when she woke up in the morning, and saw what was beside her, she was very happy. Then she resolved to pretend that it was her own.

So she told her women, that she had borne the child, and they called him Gwri of the Golden Hair.

The boy baby grew up fast, and when only two years old, was as strong as most children are at six.

Soon he was able to ride the colt that had been born on the May night, and the two were as playmates together.

Now it chanced, the man had heard the tale of Queen Rhiannon, wife of Powell, Prince of Dyfed. She had become the mother of a baby boy, but it was stolen from her at night.

The six serving women, whose duty it was to attend to the Queen, and guard her child, were lazy and had neglected their duty. They were asleep when the baby was stolen away. To excuse themselves and be saved from punishment, they invented a lying story. They declared that Rhiannon had devoured the child, her own baby.

The wise men of the Court believed the story which the six wicked women had told, and Rhiannon, the Queen, though innocent, was condemned to do penance. She was to serve as a porter to carry visitors and their baggage from out doors into the castle.

Every day, for many months, through the hours of daylight, she stood in public disgrace in front of the castle of Narberth, at the stone block, on which riders on horses dismounted from the saddle. When anyone got off at the gate, she had to carry him or her on her back into the hall.

As the boy grew up, his foster father scanned his features closely, and it was not long before he made up his mind that Powell was his father and Rhiannon was his mother.

One day, with the boy riding on his colt, and with two knights keeping him company, the owner of the Co-ed mare came near the castle of Narberth.

There they saw the beautiful Rhiannon sitting on the horse block at the gate.

When they were about to dismount from their horses, the lovely woman spoke to them thus:

"Chieftains, go no further thus. I will carry everyone of you on my back, into the palace."

Seeing their looks of astonishment, she explained:

"This is my penance for the charge brought against me of slaying my son and devouring him."

One and all the four refused to be carried and went into the castle on their own feet. There Powell, the prince, welcomed them and made a feast in their honor. It being night, Rhiannon sat beside him.

After dinner when the time for story telling had come, the chief guest told the tale of his mare and the colt, and how he cut the clawed hand, and then found the boy on the doorstep.

Then to the joy and surprise of all, the owner of the Co-ed mare, putting the golden-haired boy before Rhiannon, cried out:

"Behold lady, here is thy son, and whoever they were who told the story and lied about your devouring your own child, have done you a grievous wrong."

Everyone at the table looked at the boy, and all recognized the lad at once as the child of Powell and Rhiannon.

"Here ends my trouble (pryderi)," cried out Rhiannon.

Thereupon one of the chiefs said:

"Well hast thou named thy child 'Trouble,'" and henceforth Pryderi was his name.

Soon it was made known, by the vision and word of the bards and seers, that all the mischief had been wrought by wicked fairies, and that the six serving women had been under their spell, when they lied about the Queen. Powell, the castle-lord, was so happy that he offered the man of Co-ed rich gifts of horses, jewels and dogs.

But this good man felt repaid in delivering a pure woman and loving mother from undeserved shame and disgrace, by wisdom and honesty according to common duty.

As for Pryderi, he was educated as a king's son ought to be, in all gentle arts and was trained in all manly exercises.

After his father died, Pryderi became ruler of the realm. He married Kieva the daughter of a powerful chieftain, who had a pedigree as long as the bridle used to drive a ten-horse chariot. It reached back to Prince Casnar of Britain.

Pryderi had many adventures, which are told in the Mabinogian, which is the great storehouse of Welsh hero, wonder, and fairy tales.

6

THE GOLDEN HARP

Morgan is one of the oldest names in Cymric land. It means one who lives near the sea.

Every day, for centuries past, tens of thousands of Welsh folks have looked out on the great blue plain of salt water.

It is just as true, also, that there are all sorts of Morgans. One of these named Taffy, was like nearly all Welshmen, in that he was very fond of singing.

The trouble in his case, however, was that no one but him-self loved to hear his voice, which was very disagreeable. Yet of the sounds which he himself made with voice or instrument, he was an intense admirer. Nobody could persuade him that his music was poor and his voice rough. He always refused to im-prove.

Now in Wales, the bard, or poet, who makes up his poetry or song as he goes along, is a very important person, and it is not well to offend one of these gentlemen. In French, they call such a person by a very long name—the improvisator.

These poets have sharp tongues and often say hard things about people whom they do not like. If they used whetstones, or stropped their tongues on leather, as men do their razors, to give them a keener edge, their words could not cut more ter-ribly.

Now, on one occasion, Morgan had offended one of these bards. It was while the poetic gentleman was passing by Taffy's house. He heard the jolly fellow inside singing, first at the top and then at the bottom of the scale. He would drop his voice down on the low notes and then again rise to the highest until it ended in a screech.

Someone on the street asked the poet how he liked the music which he had heard inside.

"Music?" replied the bard with a sneer. "Is that what Morgan is trying? Why! I thought it was first the lowing of an aged cow, and then the yelping of a blind dog, unable to find its way. Do you call that music?"

The truth was that when the soloist had so filled himself with strong ale that his brain was fuddled, then it was hard to tell just what kind of a noise he was making. It took a wise man to discover the tune, if there was any.

One evening, when Morgan thought his singing unusually fine, and felt sorry that no one heard him, he heard a knock.

Instead of going to the door to inquire, or welcome the visitor, he yelled out "Come in!"

The door opened and there stood three tired looking strangers. They appeared to be travelers. One of them said:

"Kind sir, we are weary and worn, and would be glad of a morsel of bread. If you can give us a little food, we shall not trouble you further."

"Is that all?" said Morgan. "See there the loaf and the cheese, with a knife beside them. Take what you want, and fill your bags. No man shall ever say that Taffy Morgan denied anyone food, when he had any himself."

Whereupon the three travellers sat down and began to eat.

Meanwhile, without being invited to do so, their host began to sing for them.

Now the three travellers were fairies in disguise. They were journeying over the country, from cottage to cottage, visiting the people. They came to reward all who gave them a welcome and were kind to them, but to vex and play tricks upon those who were stingy, bad tempered, or of sour disposition. Turning to Taffy before taking leave, one of them said:

"You have been good to us and we are grateful. Now what can we do for you? We have power to grant anything you may desire. Please tell us what you would like most."

At this, Taffy looked hard in the faces of the three strangers, to see if one of them was the bard who had likened his voice in its ups and downs to a cow and a blind dog. Not seeing any familiar face, he plucked up his courage, and said:

"If you are not making fun of me, I'll take from you a harp. And, if I can have my wish in full, I want one that will play only lively tunes. No sad music for me!"

Here Morgan stopped. Again he searched their faces, to see if they were laughing at him and then proceeded.

"And something else, if I can have it; but it's really the same thing I am asking for."

"Speak on, we are ready to do what you wish," answered the leader.

"I want a harp, which, no matter how badly I may play, will sound out sweet and jolly music."

"Say no more," said the leader, who waved his hand. There was a flood of light, and, to Morgan's amazement, there stood on the floor a golden harp.

But where were the three travelers? They had disappeared in a flash.

Hardly able to believe his own eyes, it now dawned upon him that his visitors were fairies.

He sat down, back of the harp, and made ready to sweep the strings. He hardly knew whether or not he touched the instrument, but there rolled out volumes of lively music, as if the harp itself were mad. The tune was wild and such as would set the feet of young folks agoing, even in church.

As Taffy's fingers seemed every moment to become more skillful, the livelier the music increased, until the very dishes rattled on the cupboard, as if they wanted to join in. Even the chair looked as if about to dance.

Just then, Morgan's wife and some neighbors entered the

house. Immediately, the whole party, one and all, began dancing in the jolliest way. For hours, they kept up the mad whirl. Yet all the while, Taffy seemed happier and the women the merrier.

No telegraph ever carried the news faster, all over the region, that Morgan had a wonderful harp.

All the grass in front of the house, was soon worn away by the crowds, that came to hear and dance. As soon as Taffy touched the harp strings, the feet of everyone, young and old, began shuffling, nor could anyone stop, so long as Morgan played. Even very old, lame and one-legged people joined in. Several old women, whom nobody had ever prevailed upon to get out of their chairs, were cured of their rheumatism. Such unusual exercise was severe for them, but it seemed to be healthful.

A shrewd monk, the business manager of the monastery near by, wanted to buy Morgan's house, set up a sanatarium and advertise it as a holy place. He hoped thus to draw pilgrims to it and get for it a great reputation as a healing place for the lame and the halt, the palsied and the rheumatic. Thus the monastery would be enriched and all the monks get fat.

But Taffy was a happy-go-lucky fellow, who cared little about money and would not sell; for, with his harp, he enjoyed both fun and fame.

One day, in the crowd that stood around his door waiting to begin to hop and whirl, Morgan espied the bard who had compared his voice to a cow and a cur. The bard had come to see whether the stories about the harp were true or not.

He found to his own discomfort what was the fact and the reality, which were not very convenient for him. As soon as the harp music began, his feet began to go up, and his legs to kick and whirl. The more Morgan played, the madder the dance and the wilder the antics of the crowd, and in these the bard had to join, for he could not help himself. Soon they all began to spin round and round on the flagstones fronting the door, as if crazy. They broke the paling of the garden fence. They came into the house and knocked over the chairs and sofa, even when they cracked their shins against the wood. They bumped their heads against the walls and ceiling, and some even scrambled over the roof and down again. The bard could no more stop his weary legs than could the other lunatics.

To Morgan his revenge was so sweet, that he kept on until the bard's legs snapped, and he fell down on top of people that had tumbled from shear weariness, because no more strength was left in them.

Meanwhile, Morgan laughed until his jaws were tired and his stomach muscles ached.

But no sooner did he take his fingers off the strings, to rest them, than he opened his eyes in wonder; for in a flash the harp had disappeared.

He had made a bad use of the fairies' gift, and they were displeased. So both the monk and Morgan felt sorry.

Yet the grass grew again when the quondam harper and singer ceased desolating the air with his quavers. The air seemed sweeter to breathe, because of the silence.

However, the fairies kept on doing good to the people of good will, and to-day some of the sweetest singers in Wales come from the poorest homes.

7

THE GREAT RED DRAGON OF WALES

Every old country that has won fame in history and built up a civilization of its own, has a national flower. Besides this, some living creature, bird, or beast, or, it may be, a fish is on its flag. In places of honor, it stands as the emblem of the nation; that is, of the people, apart from the land they live on. Besides flag and symbol, it has a motto. That of Wales is: "Awake: It is light."

Now because the glorious stories of Wales, Scotland and Ireland have been nearly lost in that of mighty England, men have at times, almost forgotten about the leek, the thistle, and the shamrock, which stand for the other three divisions of the British Isles.

Yet each of these peoples has a history as noble as that of which the rose and the lion are the emblems. Each has also its patron saint and civilizer. So we have Saint George, Saint David, Saint Andrew, and Saint Patrick, all of them white-souled heroes. On the union flag, or standard of the United Kingdom, we see their three crosses.

The lion of England, the harp of Ireland, the thistle of Scotland, and the Red Dragon of Wales represent the four peoples in the British Isles, each with its own speech, traditions, and emblems; yet all in unity and in loyalty, none excelling the Welsh, whose symbol is the Red Dragon. In classic phrase, we talk of Albion, Scotia, Cymry, and Hibernia.

But why red? Almost all the other dragons in the world are white, or yellow, green or purple, blue, or pink. Why a fiery red color like that of Mars?

Borne on the banners of the Welsh archers, who in old days won the battles of Crecy and Agincourt, and now seen on the crests on the town halls and city flags, in heraldry, and in art, the red dragon is as rampant, as when King Arthur sat with His Knights at the Round Table.

The Red Dragon has four three-toed claws, a long, barbed tongue, and tail ending like an arrow head. With its wide wings unfolded, it guards those ancient liberties, which neither Saxon, nor Norman, nor German, nor kings on the throne, whether foolish or wise, have ever been able to take away. No people on earth combine so handsomely loyal freedom and the larger patriotism, or hold in purer loyalty to the union of hearts and hands in the British Empire, which the sovereign represents, as do the Welsh.

The Welsh are the oldest of the British peoples. They preserve the language of the Druids, bards, and chiefs, of primeval ages which go back and far beyond any royal line in Europe, while most of their fairy tales are pre-ancient and beyond the dating.

Why the Cymric dragon is red, is thus told, from times beyond human record.

It was in those early days, after the Romans in the south had left the island, and the Cymric king, Vortigern, was hard pressed by the Picts and Scots of the north. To his aid, he invited over from beyond the North Sea, or German Ocean, the tribes called the Long Knives, or Saxons, to help him.

But once on the big island, these friends became enemies and would not go back. They wanted to possess all Britain.

Vortigern thought this was treachery. Knowing that the Long Knives would soon attack him, he called his twelve wise men together for their advice. With one voice, they advised him to retreat westward behind the mountains into Cymry. There he must build a strong fortress and there defy his enemies.

So the Saxons, who were Germans, thought they had driven the Cymry beyond the western borders of the country which was later called England, and into what they named the foreign or Welsh parts. Centuries afterwards, this land received the name of Wales.

People in Europe spoke of Galatians, Wallachians, Belgians, Walloons, Alsatians, and others as "Welsh." They called the new fruit imported from Asia walnuts, but the names "Wales" and "Welsh" were unheard of until after the fifth century.

The place chosen for the fortified city of the Cymry was among the mountains. From all over his realm, the King sent for masons and carpenters and collected the materials for building. Then, a solemn invocation was made to the gods by the Druid priests. These grand looking old men were robed in white, with long, snowy beards falling over their breasts, and they had milk-white oxen drawing their chariot. With a silver knife they cut the mistletoe from the tree-branch, hailing it as a sign of favor from God. Then with harp, music and song they dedicated the spot as a stronghold of the Cymric nation.

Then the King set the diggers to work. He promised a rich reward to those men of the pick and shovel who should dig the fastest and throw up the most dirt, so that the masons could, at the earliest moment, begin their part of the work.

But it all turned out differently from what the king expected. Some dragon, or powerful being underground, must have been offended by this invasion of his domain; for, the next morning, they saw that everything in the form of stone, timber, iron or tools, had disappeared during the night. It looked as if an earthquake had swallowed them all up.

Both king and seers, priests and bards, were greatly puzzled at this. However, not being able to account for it, and the Saxons likely to march on them at any time, the sovereign set the diggers at work and again collected more wood and stone.

This time, even the women helped, not only to cook the food, but to drag the logs and stones. They were even ready to cut off their beautiful long hair to make ropes, if necessary.

But in the morning, all had again disappeared, as if swept by a tempest. The ground was bare.

Nevertheless, all hands began again, for all hearts were united.

For the third time, the work proceeded. Yet when the sun rose next morning, there was not even a trace of either material or labor.

What was the matter? Had some dragon swallowed everything up?

Vortigern again summoned his twelve wise men, to meet in council, and to inquire concerning the cause of the marvel and to decide what was to be done.

After long deliberation, while all the workmen and people outside waited for their verdict, the wise men agreed upon a remedy.

Now in ancient times, it was a custom, all over the world, notably in China and Japan and among our ancestors, that when a new castle or bridge was to be built, they sacrificed a human being. This was done either by walling up the victim while alive, or by mixing his or her blood with the cement used in the walls. Often it was a virgin or a little child thus chosen by lot and made to die, the one for the many.

The idea was not only to ward off the anger of the spirits of the air, or to appease the dragons under ground, but also to make the workmen do their best work faithfully, so that the foundation should be sure and the edifice withstand the storm, the wind, and the earthquake shocks.

So, nobody was surprised, or raised his eyebrows, or shook his head, or pursed up his lips, when the king announced that what the wise men declared, must be done and that quickly. Nevertheless, many a mother hugged her darling more closely to her bosom, and fathers feared for their sons or daughters, lest one of these, their own, should be chosen as the victim to be slain.

King Vortigern had the long horn blown for perfect silence, and then he spoke:

"A child must be found who was born without a father. He must be brought here and be solemnly put to death. Then his blood will be sprinkled on the ground and the citadel will be built securely."

Within an hour, swift runners were seen bounding over the Cymric hills. They were dispatched in search of a boy without a father, and a large reward was promised to the young man who found what was wanted. So into every part of the Cymric land, the searchers went.

One messenger noticed some boys playing ball. Two of them were quarreling. Coming near, he heard one say to the other:

"Oh, you boy without a father, nothing good will ever happen to you."

"This must be the one looked for," said the royal messenger to himself. So he went up to the boy, who had been thus twitted and spoke to him thus:

"Don't mind what he says." Then he prophesied great things, if he would go along with him. The boy was only too glad to go, and the next day the lad was brought before King Vortigern.

The workmen and their wives and children, numbering thousands, had assembled for the solemn ceremony of dedicating the ground by shedding the boy's blood. In strained attention the people held their breath.

The boy asked the king:

"Why have your servants brought me to this place?"

Then the sovereign told him the reason, and the boy asked:

"Who instructed you to do this?"

"My wise men told me so to do, and even the sovereign of

the land obeys his wise councilors."

"Order them to come to me, Your Majesty," pleaded the boy.

When the wise men appeared, the boy, in respectful manner, inquired of them thus:

"How was the secret of my life revealed to you? Please speak freely and declare who it was that discovered me to you."

Turning to the king, the boy added:

"Pardon my boldness, Your Majesty. I shall soon reveal the whole matter to you, but I wish first to question your advisers. I want them to tell you what is the real cause, and reveal, if they can, what is hidden here underneath the ground."

But the wise men were confounded. They could not tell and they fully confessed their ignorance.

The boy then said:

"There is a pool of water down below. Please order your men to dig for it."

At once the spades were plied by strong hands, and in a few minutes the workmen saw their faces reflected, as in a looking glass. There was a pool of clear water there.

Turning to the wise men, the boy asked before all:

"Now tell me, what is in the pool?"

As ignorant as before, and now thoroughly ashamed, the wise men were silent.

"Your Majesty, I can tell you, even if these men cannot. There are two vases in the pool."

Two brave men leaped down into the pool. They felt around and brought up two vases, as the boy had said.

Again, the lad put a question to the wise men:

"What is in these vases?"

Once more, those who professed to know the secrets of the world, even to the demanding of the life of a human being, held their tongues.

"There is a tent in them," said the boy. "Separate them, and you will find it so."

By the king's command, a soldier thrust in his hand and found a folded tent.

Again, while all wondered, the boy was in command of the situation. Everything seemed so reasonable, that all were prompt and alert to serve him.

"What a splendid chief and general, he would make, to lead us against our enemies, the 'Long Knives!'" whispered one soldier to another.

"What is in the tent?" asked the boy of the wise men.

Not one of the twelve knew what to say, and there was an almost painful silence.

"I will tell you, Your Majesty, and all here, what is in this tent. There are two serpents, one white and one red. Unfold the tent."

With such a leader, no soldier was afraid, nor did a single person in the crowd draw back? Two stalwart fellows stepped forward to open the tent.

But now, a few of the men and many of the women shrank back while those that had babies, or little folks, snatched up their children, fearing lest the poisonous snakes might wriggle towards them.

The two serpents were coiled up and asleep, but they soon showed signs of waking, and their fiery, lidless eyes glared at the people.

"Now, Your Majesty, and all here, be you the witnesses of what will happen. Let the King and wise men look in the tent."

At this moment, the serpents stretched themselves out at full length, while all fell back, giving them a wide circle to struggle in.

Then they reared their heads. With their glittering eyes flashing fire, they began to struggle with each other. The white one rose up first, threw the red one into the middle of the arena, and then pursued him to the edge of the round space.

Three times did the white serpent gain the victory over the red one.

But while the white serpent seemed to be gloating over the other for a final onset, the red one, gathering strength, erected its head and struck at the other.

The struggle went on for several minutes, but in the end the red serpent overcame the white, driving it first out of the circle, then from the tent, and into the pool, where it disappeared, while the victorious red one moved into the tent again.

When the tent flap was opened for all to see, nothing was visible except a red dragon; for the victorious serpent had turned into this great creature which combined in one new form the body and the powers of bird, beast, reptile and fish. It had wings to fly, the strongest animal strength, and could crawl, swim, and live in either water or air, or on the earth. In its body was the sum total of all life.

Then, in the presence of all the assembly, the youth turned to the wise men to explain the meaning of what had happened. But not a word did they speak. In fact, their faces were full of shame before the great crowd.

"Now, Your Majesty, let me reveal to you the meaning of this mystery."

"Speak on," said the King, gratefully.

"This pool is the emblem of the world, and the tent is that of your kingdom. The two serpents are two dragons. The white serpent is the dragon of the Saxons, who now occupy several of the provinces and districts of Britain and from sea to sea. But when they invade our soil our people will finally drive them back and hold fast forever their beloved Cymric land. But you must choose another site, on which to erect your castle."

After this, whenever a castle was to be built no more human victims were doomed to death. All the twelve men, who had wanted to keep up the old cruel custom, were treated as deceivers of the people. By the King's orders, they were all put to death and buried before all the crowd.

To-day, like so many who keep alive old and worn-out no-tions by means of deception and falsehood, these men are remembered only by the Twelve Mounds, which rise on the surface of the field hard by.

As for the boy, he became a great magician, or, as we in our age would call him, a man of science and wisdom, named Merlin. He lived long on the mountain, but when he went away with a friend, he placed all his treasures in a golden cauldron and hid them in a cave. He rolled a great stone over its mouth. Then with sod and earth he covered it all over so as to hide it from view. His purpose was to leave this his wealth for a leader, who, in some future generation, would use it for the benefit of his country, when most needed.

This special person will be a youth with yellow hair and blue eyes. When he comes to Denas, a bell will ring to invite him into the cave. The moment his foot is over the place, the stone of entrance will open of its own accord. Anyone else will be considered an intruder and it will not be possible for him to carry away the treasure.

THE TOUCH OF CLAY

Long, long ago before the Cymry came into the beautiful land of Wales, there were dark-skinned people living in caves.

In these early times there were a great many fairies of all sorts, but of very different kinds of behavior, good and bad.

It was in this age of the world that fairies got an idea riveted into their heads which nothing, not even hammers, chisels or crowbars can pry up. Neither horse power, nor hydraulic force nor sixteen-inch bombs, nor cannon balls, nor torpedoes can drive it out.

It is a settled matter of opinion in fairy land that, compared with fairies, human beings are very stupid. The fairies think that mortals are dull witted and awfully slow, when compared to the smarter and more nimble fairies, that are always up to date in doing things.

Perhaps the following story will help explain why this is.

These ancient folks who lived in caves, could not possibly know some things that are like A B C to the fairies of to-day. For the Welsh fairies, King Puck and Queen Mab, know all about what is in the telegraphs, submarine cables and wireless telegraphy of to-day. Puck would laugh if you should say that a telephone was any new thing to him. Long ago, in Shakespeare's time, he boasted that he could "put a girdle round the earth in forty minutes." Men have been trying ever since to catch up with him, but they have not gone ahead of him yet.

If, only three hundred years ago, this were the case, what must have been Puck's fun, when he saw men in the early days, working so hard to make even a clay cup or saucer. These people who slept and ate in cave boarding-houses, knew nothing of metals, or how to make iron or brass tools, wire, or machines, or how to touch a button and light up a whole room, which even a baby can now do.

There is one thing that we, who have traveled in many fairy lands, have often noticed and told our friends, the little folks, and that is this:

All the fairies we ever knew are very slow to change either their opinions, or their ways, or their fashions. Like many mortals, they think a great deal of their own notions. They imagine that the only way to do a thing is in that which they say is the right one.

So it came to pass that even when the Cymric folk gave up wearing the skins of animals, and put on pretty clothes woven on a loom, and ate out of dishes, instead of clam shells, there were still some fairies that kept to the notions and fashions of the cave days. To one of these, came trouble because of this failing.

Now there was once a pretty nymph, who lived in the Red Lake, to which a young and handsome farmer used to come to catch fish. One misty day, when the lad could see only a few feet before him, a wind cleared the air and blew away the fog. Then he saw near him a little old man, standing on a ladder. He was hard at work in putting a thatched roof on a hut which he had built.

A few minutes later, as the mist rose and the breezes blew, the farmer could see no house, but only the ripplings of water on the lake's surface.

Although he went fishing often, he never again saw anything unusual, during the whole summer.

On one hot day in the early autumn, while he stopped to let

his horse drink, he looked and saw a very lovely face on the water. Wondering to whom it might belong, there rose up before him the head and shoulders of a most beautiful woman. She was so pretty that he had two tumbles. He fell off his horse and he fell in love with her at one and the same time.

Rushing toward the lovely vision, he put out his arms at that spot where he had seen her, but only to embrace empty air. Then he remembered that love is blind. So he rubbed his eyes, to see if he could discern anything. Yet though he peered down into the water, and up over the hills, he could not see her anywhere.

But he soon found out to his joy that his eyes were all right, for in another place, the face, flower-crowned hair, and her reflection in the water came again. Then his desire to possess the damsel was doubled. But again, she disappeared, to rise again somewhere else.

Five times he was thus tantalized and disappointed. She rose up, and quickly disappeared.

It seemed as though she meant only to tease him. So he rode home sorrowing, and scarcely slept that night.

Early morning, found the lovelorn youth again at the lake side, but for hours he watched in vain. He had left his home too excited to have eaten his usual breakfast, which greatly surprised his housekeeper. Now he pulled out some sweet apples, which a neighbor had given him, and began to munch them, while still keeping watch on the waters.

No sooner had the aroma of the apples fallen on the air, than the pretty lady of the lake bobbed up from beneath the surface, and this time quite near him. She seemed to have lost all fear, for she asked him to throw her one of the apples.

"Please come, pretty maid, and get it yourself," cried the farmer. Then he held up the red apple, turning it round and round before her, to tempt her by showing its glossy surface and rich color.

Apparently not afraid, she came up close to him and took

the apple from his left hand. At once, he slipped his strong right arm around her waist, and hugged her tight. At this, she screamed loudly.

Then there appeared in the middle of the lake the old man, he had seen thatching the roof by the lake shore. This time, besides his long snowy beard, he had on his head a crown of water lilies.

"Mortal," said the venerable person. "That is my daughter you are clasping. What do you wish to do with her?"

At once, the farmer broke out in passionate appeal to the old man that she might become his wife. He promised to love her always, treat her well, and never be rough or cruel to her.

The old father listened attentively. He was finally convinced that the farmer would make a good husband for his lovely daughter. Yet he was very sorry to lose her, and he solemnly laid one condition upon his future son-in-law.

He was never under any pretense, or in any way, to strike her with clay, or with anything made or baked from clay. Any blow with that from which men made pots and pans, and jars and dishes, or in fact, with earth of any sort, would mean the instant loss of his wife. Even if children were born in their home, the mother would leave them, and return to fairy land under the lake, and be forever subject to the law of the fairies, as before her marriage.

The farmer was very much in love with his pretty prize, and as promises are easily made, he took oath that no clay should ever touch her.

They were married and lived very happily together. Years passed and the man was still a good husband and lover. He kept up the habit which he had learned from a sailor friend. Every night, when far from home and out on the sea, he and his mates used to drink this toast; "Sweethearts and wives: may every sweetheart become a wife and every wife remain a sweetheart, and every husband continue a lover."

So he proved that though a husband he was still a lover, by

always doing what she asked him and more. When the children were born and grew up, their father told them about their mother's likes and dislikes, her tastes and her wishes, and warned them always to be careful. So it was altogether a very happy family.

One day, the wife and mother said to her husband, that she had a great longing for apples. She would like to taste some like those which he long ago gave her. At once, the good man dropped what he was doing and hurried off to his neighbor, who had first presented him with a trayful of these apples.

The farmer not only got the fruit, but he also determined that he would plant a tree and thus have apples for his wife, whenever she wanted them. So he bought a fine young sapling, to set in his orchard, for the children to play under and to keep his pantry full of the fine red-cheeked fruit. At this his wife was delighted.

So happy enough—in fact, too merry to think of anything else, they, both husband and wife, proceeded to set the sapling in the ground. She held the tree, while he dug down to make the hole deep enough to make sure of its growing.

But farmers are sometimes very superstitious. They even believe in luck, though not in Puck. Some of them have faith in what the almanac, and the patent medicine may say, and in planting potatoes according to the moon, but they scout the idea of there being any fairies.

With the farmer, this had become a fixed state of mind and now it brought him to grief, as we shall see. For though he remembered what his wife liked and disliked, and recalled what her father had told him, he had forgotten that she was a fairy.

With this farmer and other Welsh mortals, it had become a habit, when planting a young tree, to throw the last shovelful of earth over the left shoulder. This was for good luck. The farmer was afraid to break such a good custom, as he thought it to be.

So merrily he went to work, forgetting everything in his adherence to habit. He became so absorbed in his job, that he did not look where his spadeful went, and it struck his dear wife full in the breast.

At that moment, she cried out bitterly, not in pain, but in sorrow. Then she started to run towards the lake. At the shore, she called out, "Good-by, dear, dear husband." Then, leaping into the water, she was never seen again and all his tears and those of the children never brought her back.

The Touch of Iron

Ages ago, before the Cymry rowed in their coracles across the sea, there was a race of men already in the Land of Honey, as Great Britain was then called.

These ancient people, who lived in caves, did not know how to build houses or to plow the ground. They had no idea that they could get their food out of the earth. As for making bread and pies, cookies and goodies, from what grew from the soil, they never heard of such a thing. They were not acquainted with the use of fire for melting copper, nor did they know how to get iron out of the ore, to make knives and spears, arrow heads and swords, and armor and helmets.

All they could do was to mold clay, so as to make things to cook with and hold milk, or water. When they baked this soft stuff in the fire, they found they had pots, pans and dishes as hard as stone, though these were easily broken.

To hunt the deer, or fight the wolves and bears, they fash-ioned clubs of wood. For javelins and arrows, they took hard stone like flint and chipped it to points and sharpened it with edges. This was the time which men now call the Stone Age. When the men went to war, their weapons were wholly of wood or stone.

They had not yet learned to weave the wool of the sheep into warm clothing, but they wore the skins of animals. Each one of the caves, in which they lived, was a general boarding house, for dogs and pigs, as well as people.

When a young man of one tribe wanted a wife, he sallied out secretly into another neighborhood. There he lay in wait for a girl to come along. He then ran away with her, and back to his own daddy's cave.

By and by, when the Cymry came into the land, they had iron tools and better weapons of war. Then there were many and long battles and the aborigines were beaten many times.

So the cave people hated everything made of iron. Anyone of the cave people, girls or boys, who had picked up iron ornaments, and were found wearing or using iron tools, or buying anything of iron from the cave people's enemies, was looked upon as a rascal, or a villain, or even as a traitor and was driven out of the tribe.

However, some of the daughters of the cave men were so pretty and had such rosy cheeks, and lovely bodies, and beautiful, long hair, that quite often the Cymric youth fell in love with them.

Many of the cave men's daughters were captured and became wives of the Cymry and mothers of children. In course of ages, their descendants helped to make the bright, witty, song-loving Welsh people.

Now the fairies usually like things that are old, and they are very slow to alter the ancient customs, to which they have been used; for, in the fairy world, there is no measure of time, nor any clocks, watches, or bells to strike the hours, and no almanacs or calendars.

The fairies cannot understand why ladies change the fashions so often, and the men their ways of doing things. They wonder why beards are fashionable at one time; then, moustaches long or short, at another; or smooth faces when razors are cheap. Most fairies like to keep on doing the same thing in the old way. They enjoy being like the mountains, which stand; or the sea, that rolls; or the sun, that rises and sets every day and forever. They never get tired of repeating to-morrow what they did yesterday. They are very different from the people that are always wanting something else, and even cry if they cannot have it.

That is the reason why the fairies did not like iron, or to see men wearing iron hats and clothes, called helmets and armor, when they went to war. They no more wanted to be touched by iron than by filth, or foul disease. They hated knives, stirrups, scythes, swords, pots, pans, kettles, or this metal in any form, whether sheet, barbed wire, lump or pig iron.

Now there was a long, pretty stretch of water, near which lived a handsome lad, who loved nothing better than to go out on moonlight nights and see the fairies dance, or listen to their music. This youth fell in love with one of these fairies, whose beauty was great beyond description. At last, unable to control his passion, he rushed into the midst of the fairy company, seized the beautiful one, and rushed back to his home, with his prize in his arms. This was in true cave-man fashion. When the other fairies hurried to rescue her, they found the man's house shut. They dared not touch the door, for it was covered over with iron studs and bands, and bolted with the metal which they most abhorred.

The young man immediately began to make love to the fairy maid, hoping to win her to be his wife. For a long time she refused, and moped all day and night. While weeping many salt water tears, she declared that she was too homesick to live.

Nevertheless the lover persevered. Finding herself locked in with iron bars, while gratings, bolts and creaking hinges were all about her, and unable to return to her people, the fairy first thought out a plan of possible escape. Then she agreed to become the man's wife. She resolved, at least, that, without touching it, she should oil all the iron work, and stop the noise.

She was a smart fairy, and was sure she could outwit the man, even if he were so strong, and had every sort of iron everywhere in order to keep her as it were in a prison. So, pretending she loved him dearly, she said: "I will not be your wife, but, if you can find out my name, I shall gladly become your servant."

"Easily won," thought the lover to himself. Yet the game was a harder one to play than he supposed. It was like playing Blind Man's Buff, or Hunt the Slipper. Although he made guesses of every name he could think of, he was never "hot" and got no nearer to the thing sought than if his eyes were bandaged. All the time, he was deeper and deeper in love with the lovely fairy maid.

But one night, on returning home, he saw in a turf bog, a group of fairies sitting on a log. At once, he thought, they might be talking about their lost sister. So he crept up quite near them, and soon found that he had guessed right. After a long discussion, finding themselves still at a loss, as to how to recover her, he heard one of them sigh and say, "Oh, Siwsi, my sister, how can you live with a mortal?"

"Enough," said the young man to himself. "I've got it." Then, crawling away noiselessly, he ran back all the way to his house, and unlocked the door. Once inside the room, he called out his servant's name—"Siwsi! Siwsi!"

Astonished at hearing her name, she cried out, "What mortal has betrayed me? For, surely no fairy would tell on me? Alas, my fate, my fate!"

But in her own mind, the struggle and the fear were over. She had bravely striven to keep her fairyhood, and in the battle of wits, had lost.

She would not be wife, but what a wise, superb and faithful servant she made!

Everything prospered under her hand. The house and the farm became models. Not twice, but three times a day, the cows, milked by her, yielded milk unusually rich in cream. In the market, her butter excelled, in quality and price, all others.

Meanwhile, the passion of the lover abated not one jot, or for an instant. His perseverance finally won. She agreed to become his wife; but only on one condition.

"You must never strike me with iron," she said. "If you do, I'll feel free to leave you, and go back to my relatives in the fairy family."

A hearty laugh from the happy lover greeted this remark, made by the lovely creature, once his servant, but now his betrothed. He thought that the condition was very easy to obey.

So they were married, and no couple in all the land seemed to be happier. Once, twice, the cradle was filled. It rocked with new treasures that had life, and were more dear than farm, or home, or wealth in barns or cattle, cheese and butter. A boy and a girl were theirs. Then the mother's care was unremitting, day and night.

Even though the happy father grew richer every year, and bought farm after farm, until he owned five thousand acres, he valued, more than these possessions, his lovely wife and his beautiful children.

Yet this very delight and affection made him less vigilant; yes, even less careful concerning the promise he had once given to his fairy wife, who still held to the ancient ideas of the Fairy Family in regard to iron.

One of his finest mares had given birth to a filly, which, when the day of the great fair came, he determined to sell at a high price.

So with a halter on his arm, he went out to catch her.

But she was a lively creature, so frisky that it was much like his first attempt to win his fairy bride. It almost looked as if she were a cave girl running away from a lover, who had a lasso in his hand. The lively and frolicsome beast scampered here and there, grazing as she stopped, as if she were determined to put off her capture as long as possible.

So, calling to his wife, the two of them together, tried their skill to catch the filly. This time, leaving the halter in the house, the man took bit and bridle, and the two managed to get the pretty creature into a corner; but, when they had almost captured her, away she dashed again.

By this time, the man was so vexed that he lost his temper; and he who does that, usually loses the game, while he who controls the wrath within, wins. Mad as a flaming fire, he lost his brains also and threw bit and bridle and the whole harness after the fleet animal.

Alas! alas! the wife had started to run after the filly and the iron bit struck her on the cheek. It did not hurt, but he had broken his vow.

Now came the surprise of his life. It was as if, at one moment, a flash of lightning had made all things bright; and then in another second was inky darkness. He saw this lovely wife, one moment active and fleet as a deer. In another, in the twinkling of an eye, nothing was there. She had vanished. After this, there was a lonely home, empty of its light and cheer.

But by living with human beings, a new idea and form of life had transformed this fairy, and a new spell was laid on her. Mother-love had been awakened in her heart. Henceforth, though the law of the fairy world would not allow her to touch again the realm of earth, she, having once been wife and parent, could not forget the babies born of her body. So, making a sod raft, a floating island, she came up at night, and often, while these three mortals lived, this fairy mother would spend hours tenderly talking to her husband and her two children, who were now big boy and girl, as they stood on the lake shore.

On his part, the father did not think it "an ideal arrangement," as some modern married folks do, to be thus separated, wife and husband, one from the other; but by her coming as near as could be allowed, she showed her undying love. Even today, good people sometimes see a little island floating on the lake, and this, they point out as the place where the fairy mother was wont to come and hold converse with her dear ones. When they merrily eat the pink delicacy, called "floating island," moving it about with a spoon on its yellow lake of eggs and cream, they call this "the Fairy Mother's rocking chair."

The Maiden of the Green Forest

Many a palace lies under the waves that wash Cymric land, for the sea has swallowed up more than one village, and even cities.

When Welsh fairies yield to their mortal lovers and consent to become their wives, it is always on some condition or promise. Sometimes there are several of these, which the fairy ladies compel their mortal lovers to pledge them, before they agree to become wives. In fact, the fairies in Cymric land are among the most exacting of any known.

A prince named Benlli, of the Powys region, found this out to his grief, for he had always supposed that wives could be had simply for the asking. All that a man need say, to the girl to whom he took a fancy, was this: "Come along with me, and be my bride," and then she would say, "Thank you, I'll come," and the two would trot off together. This was the man's notion.

Now Benlli was a wicked old fellow. He was already married, but wrinkles had gathered on his wife's face. She had a faded, washed-out look, and her hair was thinning out. She would never be young again, and he was tired of her, and wanted a mate with fresh rosy cheeks, and long, thick hair. He was quite ready to fall in love with such a maiden, whenever his eyes should light upon her.

One day, he went out hunting in the Green Forest. While

waiting for a wild boar to rush out, there rode past him a young woman whose beauty was dazzling. He instantly fell in love with her.

The next day, while on horseback, at the same opening in the forest, the same maiden reappeared; but it was only for a moment, and then she vanished.

Again, on the third day, the prince rode out to the appointed place, and again the vision of beauty was there. He rode up to her and begged her to come and live with him at his palace.

"I will come and be your wedded wife on three conditions: You must put away the wife you now have; you must permit me to leave you, one night in every seven, without following after or spying upon me; and you must not ask me where I go or what I do. Swear to me that you will do these three things. Then, if you keep your promises unbroken, my beauty shall never change, no, not until the tall vegetable flag-reeds wave and the long green rushes grow in your hall."

The Prince of Powys was quite ready to swear this oath and he solemnly promised to observe the three conditions. So the Maid of the Green Forest went to live with him.

"But what of his old wife?" one asks.

Ah! he had no trouble from that quarter, for when the newly-wedded couple arrived at the castle, she had already disappeared.

Happy, indeed, were the long bright days, which the prince and his new bride spent together, whether in the castle, or out doors, riding on horseback, or in hunting the deer. Every day, her beauty seemed diviner, and she more lovely. He lavished various gifts upon her, among others that of a diadem of beryl and sapphire. Then he put on her finger a diamond ring worth what was a very great sum—a king's ransom. In the Middle Ages, monarchs as well as nobles were taken prisoners in battle and large amounts of money had to be paid to get them back again. So a king's ransom is what Benlli paid for his wife's diamond ring. He loved her so dearly that he never suspected for a moment that he would ever have any trouble in keeping his three promises.

But without variety, life has no spice, and monotony wearies the soul. After nine years had passed, and his wife absented herself every Friday night, he began to wonder why it could be. His curiosity, to know the reason for her going away, so increased that it so wore on him that he became both miserable in himself and irritable toward others. Everybody in the castle noticed the change in their master, and grieved over it.

One night, he invited a learned monk from the white monastery, not far away, to come and take dinner with him. The table in the great banqueting hall was spread with the most delicious viands, the lights were magnificent, and the music gay.

But Wyland, the monk, was a man of magic and could see through things. He noticed that some secret grief was preying upon the Prince's mind. He discerned that, amidst all this splendor, he, Benlli, the lord of the castle, was the most miserable person within its walls. So Wyland went home, resolved to call again and find out what was the trouble.

When they met, some days later, Wyland's greeting was this:

"Christ save thee, Benlli! What secret sorrow clouds thy brow? Why so gloomy?"

Benlli at once burst out with the story of how he met the Maid of the Green Forest, and how she became his wife on three conditions.

"Think of it," said Benlli, groaning aloud. "When the owls cry and the crickets chirp, my wife leaves my bed, and until the daystar appears, I lie alone, torn with curiosity, to know where she is, and what she is doing. I fall again into heavy sleep, and do not awake until sunrise, when I find her by my side again. It is all such a mystery, that the secret lies heavy on my soul. Despite all my wealth, and my strong castle, with feasting and music by night and hunting by day, I am the most miserable man in Cymric land. No beggar is more wretched than I."

Wyland, the monk, listened and his eyes glittered. There came into his head the idea of enriching the monastery. He saw his chance, and improved it at once. He could make money by solving the secret for a troubled soul.

"Prince Benlli," said he, "if you will bestow upon the monks of the White Minster, one tenth of all the flocks that feed with-in your domain, and one tenth of all that flows into the vaults of your palace, and hand over the Maiden of the Green Forest to me, I shall warrant that your soul will be at peace and your troubles end."

To all this, Prince Benlli agreed, making solemn promise. Then the monk Wyland took his book, leather bound, and kept shut by means of metal clasps, and hid himself in the cranny of a rock near the Giant's Cave, from which there was entrance down into Fairyland.

He had not long to wait, for soon, with a crown on her head, a lady, royally arrayed, passed by out of the silvery moonlight into the dark cave. It was none other than the Maiden of the Green Forest.

Now came a battle of magic and spells, as between the monk's own and those of the Green Forest Maiden. He moved forward to the mouth of the cave. Then summoning into his presence the spirits of the air and the cave, he informed them as to Benlli's vow to enrich the monastery, and to deliver the Green Forest Maiden to himself. Then, calling aloud, he said:

"Let her forever be, as she now appears, and never leave my side."

"Bring her, before the break of day, to the cross near the town of the White Minster, and there will I wed her, and swear to make her my own."

Then, by the power of his magic, he made it impossible for any person or power to recall or hinder the operation of these words. Leaving the cave's mouth, in order to be at the cross, be-fore day should dawn, the first thing he met was a hideous ogress, grinning and rolling her bleared red eyes at him. On her head seemed what was more like moss, than hair. She stretched out a long bony finger at him. On it, flashed the splendid diamond, which Benlli had given his bride, the beautiful Maid of the Green Forest.

"Take me to thy bosom, monk Wyland," she shrieked, laughing hideously and showing what looked like green snags in her mouth. "For I am the wife you are sworn to wed. Thirty years ago, I was Benlli's blooming bride. When my beauty left me, his love flew out of the window. Now I am a foul ogress, but magic makes me young again every seventh night. I promised that my beauty should last until the tall flag reeds and the long green rushes grow in his hall."

Amazed at her story, Wyland drew in his breath.

"And this promise, I have kept. It is already fulfilled. Your spell and mine are both completed. Yours brought to him the peace of the dead. Mine made the river floods rush in. Now, waters lap to and fro among the reeds and rushes that grow in the banqueting hall, which is now sunk deep below the earth. With the clash of our spells, no charm can redress our fate.

"Come then and take me as thy bride, for oath and spell have both decreed it as thy reward. As Benlli's promise to you is fulfilled, for the waters flow in the palace vaults, the pike and the dare (fish) feed there."

So, caught in his own dark, sordid plot, the monk, who played conjurer, had become the victim of his own craft.

They say that Wyland's Cross still recalls the monk, while fishermen on the Welsh border, can, on nights with smooth water, see towers and chimneys far below, sunk deep beneath the waves.

THE TREASURE STONE OF THE FAIRIES

The Gruffyds were one of the largest of the Welsh tribes. To-day, it is said that in Britain one man in every forty has this, as either his first, middle, or last name. It means "hero" or "brave man," and as far back as the ninth century, the word is found in the Book of Saint Chad.

The monks, who derived nearly every name from the Latin, insisted the word meant Great Faith.

Another of the most common of Welsh personal names was William; which, when that of a father's son, was written Williams and was only the Latin for Gild Helm, or Golden Helmet.

Long ago, when London was a village and Cardiff only a hamlet, there was a boy of this name, who tended sheep on the hill sides. His father was a hard working farmer, who every year tried to coax to grow out of the stony ground some oats, barley, leeks and cabbage. In summer, he worked hard, from the first croak of the raven to the last hoot of the owl, to provide food for his wife and baby daughter. When his boy was born, he took him to the church to be christened Gruffyd, but every body called him "Gruff." In time several little sisters came to keep the boy company.

His mother always kept her cottage, which was painted pink, very neat and pretty, with vines covering the outside, while flowers bloomed indoors. These were set in pots and on shelves near the latticed windows. They seemed to grow finely, because so good a woman loved them. The copper door-sill was kept bright, and the broad borders on the clay floor, along the walls, were always fresh with whitewash. The pewter dishes on the sideboard shone as if they were moons, and the china cats on the mantle piece, in silvery luster, reflected both sun and candle light. Daddy often declared he could use these polished metal plates for a mirror, when he shaved his face. Puss, the pet, was always happy purring away on the hearth, as the kettle boiled to make the flummery, of sour oat jelly, which, daddy loved so well.

Mother Gruffyd was always so neat, with her black and white striped apron, her high peaked hat, with its scalloped lace and quilled fastening around her chin, her little short shawl, with its pointed, long tips, tied in a bow, and her bright red plaid petticoat folded back from her frock. Her snowy-white, rolling collar and neck cloth knotted at the top, and fringed at the ends, added fine touches to her picturesque costume.

In fact, young Gruffyd was proud of his mother and he loved her dearly. He thought no woman could be quite as sweet as she was.

Once, at the end of the day, on coming back home, from the hills, the boy met some lovely children. They were dressed in very fine clothes, and had elegant manners. They came up, smiled, and invited him to play with them. He joined in their sports, and was too much interested to take note of time. He kept on playing with them until it was pitch dark.

Among other games, which he enjoyed, had been that of "The King in his counting house, counting out his money," and "The Queen in her kitchen, eating bread and honey," and "The Girl hanging out the clothes," and "The Saucy Blackbird that snipped off her nose." In playing these, the children had aprons full of what seemed to be real coins, the size of crowns, or five-shilling pieces, each worth a dollar. These had "head and tail," beside letters on them and the boy supposed they were real.

But when he showed these to his mother, she saw at once

from their lightness, and because they were so easily bent, that they were only paper, and not silver.

She asked her boy where he had got them. He told her what a nice time he had enjoyed. Then she knew that these, his play-mates, were fairy children. Fearing that some evil might come of this, she charged him, her only son, never to go out again alone, on the mountain. She mistrusted that no good would come of making such strange children his companions.

But the lad was so fond of play, that one day, tired of seeing nothing but byre and garden, while his sisters liked to play girls' games more than those which boys cared most for, and the hills seeming to beckon him to come to them, he disobeyed, and slipped out and off to the mountains. He was soon missed and search was made for him.

Yet nobody had seen or heard of him. Though inquiries were made on every road, in every village, and at all the fairs and markets in the neighborhood, two whole years passed by, without a trace of the boy.

But early one morning of the twenty-fifth month, before breakfast, his mother, on opening the door, found him sitting on the steps, with a bundle under his arm, but dressed in the same clothes, and not looking a day older or in any way differ-ent, from the very hour he disappeared.

"Why my dear boy, where have you been, all these months, which have now run into the third year—so long a time that they have seemed to me like ages?"

"Why, mother dear, how strange you talk. I left here yester-day, to go out and to play with the children, on the hills, and we have had a lovely time. See what pretty clothes they have given me for a present." Then he opened his bundle.

But when she tore open the package, the mother was all the more sure that she was right, and that her fears had been justi-fied. In it she found only a dress of white paper. Examining it carefully, she could see neither seam nor stitches. She threw it in the fire, and again warned her son against fairy children.

But pretty soon, after a great calamity had come upon them, both father and mother changed their minds about fairies.

They had put all their savings into the venture of a ship, which had for a long time made trading voyages from Cardiff. Every year, it came back bringing great profit to the owners and shareholders. In this way, daddy was able to eke out his income, and keep himself, his wife and daughters comfortably clothed, while all the time the table was well supplied with good food. Nor did they ever turn from their door anyone who asked for bread and cheese.

But in the same month of the boy's return, bad news came that the good ship had gone down in a storm. All on board had perished, and the cargo was totally lost, in the deep sea, far from land. In fact, no word except that of dire disaster had come to hand.

Now it was a tradition, as old as the days of King Arthur, that on a certain hill a great boulder could be seen, which was quite different from any other kind of rock to be found within miles. It was partly imbedded in the earth, and beneath it, lay a great, yes, an untold treasure. The grass grew luxuriantly around this stone, and the sheep loved to rest at noon in its shadow. Many men had tried to lift, or pry it up, but in vain. The tradition, unaltered and unbroken for centuries, was to the effect, that none but a very good man could ever budge this stone. Any and all unworthy men might dig, or pull, or pry, until doomsday, but in vain. Till the right one came, the treasure was as safe as if in heaven.

But the boy's father and mother were now very poor and his sisters now grown up wanted pretty clothes so badly, that the lad hoped that he or his father might be the deserving one. He would help him to win the treasure for he felt sure that his parent would share his gains with all his friends.

Though his neighbors were not told of the generous intentions credited to the boy's father, by his loving son, they all came with horses, ropes, crowbars, and tackle, to help in the enterprise. Yet after many a long days' toil, between the sun's rising and setting, their end was failure. Every day, when darkness came on, the stone lay there still, as hard and fast as ever. So they gave up the task.

On the final night, the lad saw that father and mother, who were great lovers, were holding each other's hands, while their tears flowed together, and they were praying for patience.

Seeing this, before he fell asleep, the boy resolved that on the morrow, he would go up to the mountains, and talk to his fairy friends about the matter.

So early in the morning, he hurried to the hill tops, and going into one of the caves, met the fairies and told them his troubles. Then he asked them to give him again some of their money.

"Not this time, but something better. Under the great rock there are treasures waiting for you."

"Oh, don't send me there! For all the men and horses of our parish, after working a week, have been unable to budge the stone."

"We know that," answered the principal fairy, "but do you yourself try to move it. Then you will see what is certain to happen."

Going home, to tell what he had heard, his parents had a hearty laugh at the idea of a boy succeeding where men, with the united strength of many horses and oxen, had failed.

Yet, after brooding awhile, they were so dejected, that anything seemed reasonable. So they said, "Go ahead and try it."

Returning to the mountain, the fairies, in a band, went with him to the great rock.

One touch of his hand, and the mighty boulder trembled, like an aspen leaf in the breeze.

A shove, and the rock rolled down from the hill and crashed in the valley below.

There, underneath, were little heaps of gold and silver, which the boy carried home to his parents, who became the richest people in the country round about.

GIANT TOM AND GIANT BLUBB

Everyone who has read anything of Welsh history—though not of the sort that is written by English folks—knows also that Cornwall is, in soul, a part of Wales. Before the Romans, first, and the Saxons, next, invaded Britain, the Cymric people lived all over the island, south of Scotland.

They were the British people, and nobody ever heard the German name, "Wales," which means a foreign land; or the word "Welsh," which refers to foreigners, until men who were themselves outsiders came into Britain.

Since that time, it has been much the same, as when a British Jack Tar, when rambling in Portugal, or China, calls the natives "foreigners," and tells them to "get out of the way."

Ages ago, when the Cymric men, with their wives and little ones rowed over in their coracles, from Gallia, or the Summer Land, to Britain, the Honey Land, they came first to the promontory which we know as Cornwall; that is, the Cornu Galliae, or Walliae, which means Horn or Cape of the new country now called England. Here was a new region, rich in every kind of minerals. Ages before, the Phoenicians had named it Britain or the Land of Tin. Within the memory of men now living, Cornishmen, that is, the miners of Cornwall, on going to California, discovered gold.

In Cornwall, as part of the Cymric realm, King Arthur found and married Guinevere, his queen. It was in Cornwall, also, that Merlin was hidden. Hear the rhyme:

Marvelous Merlin is wasted away
By a wicked woman, who may she be?
For she hath pent him in a crag
   On Cornwall coast.

So it happens that thousands of "English" people in Cornwall are Welsh, by both name or descent, or have translated their names into English form, even while keeping the Welsh meaning. They are also Welsh in traits of character. Just as tens of thousands of Welsh folks, among the first settlers of New England and the American colonies are described in our histories as "English" people.

Now in early Cornwall there were many giants. Some were good but others were bad. One of these, a right fine fellow, was named Tom, and the other, a bad one, Blubb. This giant had had twenty wives, and was awfully cruel. Nobody ever knew what became of the twenty maidens he had married.

Sometimes people called the big fellow, that lived in a castle, Giant Blunderbuss, but Blubb was his name for short. He was much taller than the highest hop pole in Kent. He was made up mostly of head and stomach, for his chief idea in living was to eat. His skull was as big as a hogshead, or a push-ball, or a market wagon loaded with carrots. Indeed, it was strongly suspected by most people that the big bone box set on his shoulders was as hollow inside as a pumpkin, but that a cocoanut would hold all the brains he had. At any rate, during one of his fights with another giant, he had been given an awful thwack from the other giant's club. Then the sound made, which was heard a long distance away, was exactly like that when one pounds on an empty barrel.

Now this Giant Blubb had built a mighty castle between a big hill and a river. Under it were vaults of vast size, filled with treasures of all sorts, gold, silver, jewels and gems. There were cells, in which he kept his wives, after he had married them. It was the opinion of his neighbors, that in every case, soon after the honeymoon was over, he ate them up.

Yet, if even the devil ought to have his due; one should be fair to this human monster, and we are bound to say that Giant Blubb denied these stories as pure gossip. It is certain that such crimes as murder and cannibalism never could be proved against him.

To guard his underground treasures, he had two huge and fierce dogs, supposed to be named Catchem and Tearem. What they were really called by their master was a secret. Yet anyone who had a piece of meat ready to throw to them, and knew their names, which were pass words, could first quiet them. Then he could walk by them and get the treasure.

Besides these dogs, the only living thing left in the castle when the giant went out, was the latest Mrs. Blubb. Yet she was in constant fear of her life, lest her big husband should sometime make a meal of her. For even she had heard the story that Blubb was a cannibal and looked at all plump women simply as delicacies, exactly as a boy peers into the window of a candy shop.

What made all the country round hate this cruel giant was not wholly on account of his awful appetite. It was because he had ruined the King's High Road. Ever since the time of King Lud, whose name we read in Ludgate Hill, in London, where His Cymric Majesty had lived, this highway had been free to all. It ran all the way through Cornwall, from Penzance, and thence eastward to London and beyond.

When Giant Blubb wished to enlarge his castle, he had the walls and towers built down to the river's edge. This closed up the big road, so that people had to go far around and up over the hill, or by boat along the river. Such a roundabout way took much time and toil, and was too much trouble for all.

Everybody had to submit to this extortion, until there came along Giant Tom, of whom we shall now tell. His real name was Rolling Stone, for he never stuck long in one place at a job, and cared not a cucumber for money, or fine clothes.

This jolly fellow was very good-natured and popular, but often very lazy. His mother talked with him many times, urging him to learn a trade, or in some way make an honest living. She found it very hard to keep anything in her larder, barn, pantry, or cellar, when he was at home. He measured four feet across his shoulders and at every meal he ate what would feed three big men. But as he could do six men's work, when he had a mind to —as often he did—he was always welcome. In fact, he was too popular for his own good.

One day, when ten common fellows were trying their utmost to lift a big long log on a cart, and were unable to do it, Tom came along and told them to stand back. Then he hoisted the tree on to the wain, roped it into place, and told the cartman to drive on. Then they all cheered him, and one of them lifted his Monmouth cap and cried out, "Hurrah for Giant Tom. He's the fellow to whip Giant Blubb."

"He is! He is!" they all cried in chorus.

"Who is this Giant Blubb? Where does he live?" asked Tom, rolling up his sleeves, for he was just spoiling for a row with a fellow of his size.

Then they told the story of how the big bully had ruined the King's Highway, by building a great wall and tower across the road, to shut it up, to the grief of many honest men.

"Never mind, boys. I'll attend to his bacon," said Tom. "Leave the matter with me, and don't bother to tell the King about it."

Tom went the next day into town and hired himself out to a beer brewer to drive the wagon. Perhaps he hoped, also, while in this occupation, to keep down his thirst.

He asked the boss to give him the route that led past Giant Blubb's castle, over the old King's Highway.

The master of the brewery saw through Tom's purpose. He winked, and only said:

"Go ahead, my boy. I'll pay you double wages, if you will

open that road again; but see that Giant Blubb does not get my load of kegs, or that your carcass doesn't count with those of the twenty wives in his vaults and make twenty-one."

Again he winked his eye knowingly to his workmen. Tom drove off. He occupied all the room on the seat of the cart, which two men usually filled and left plenty of room on either side.

Cracking his whip, the new driver kept the four horses on a galloping pace, until very soon he called out "whoa," before the frowning high gateway of Giant Blubb.

Tom shouted from the depth of his lungs:

"Open the gate and let me drive through. This is the King's Highway."

The only reply, for a minute, was the barking of the curs. Then a rattling of bolts was heard, and the great gates swung wide open.

"Who are you, you impudnt fellow? Go round over the hill, or I'll thrash you," blustered Giant Blubb, in a rage.

"Better save your breath to cool your porridge, you big boaster, and come out and fight," said Tom.

"Fight? You pigmy. I'll just get a switch and whip you, as I would a bad boy."

Thereupon Giant Blubb stepped aside into the grove nearby, keeping all the while an eye on his gate, guarded by his two monstrous dogs. He selected an elm tree twenty feet high, tore it up by the roots, pulled off the branches, and peeled it for a whip. This he jerked up and down to make ready for his task of thrashing "the pigmy."

Meanwhile Giant Tom upset the wain, drew out the tongue and took off one of the wheels. Then, as if armed with spear and shield, he advanced to meet Giant Blubb. He whistled like a boy, as he went forward.

In a passion of rage, Giant Blubb lifted his elm switch to strike, but Tom warded off the blow with his wheel shield. Then he punched him in the stomach, with the wagon tongue, so hard that the big fellow slipped and rolled over in the mud:

Picking himself up, Giant Blubb, now half blind with rage, rushed against Tom, who, this time, made a lunge which planted the cart tongue inside Blubb's bowels, and knocked him over.

But Tom was not a cruel fellow, and had no desire to kill anyone. So he threw down his war tools, and tearing up a yard or two of grassy sod rolled it together, and made a plug of it, as big around as a milk churn. With this, he stopped up the big hole in Giant Blubb's huge body.

But instead of thanking Tom, Giant Blubb rushed at him again. He was in too much of a rage to see anything clearly, while Tom, perfectly cool, gave the angry monster such a kick, in the place where he kept his dinner, that he rolled over, and Tom gave him another kick. Then the plug of sod fell out of his wound.

As he was bleeding to death, Giant Blubb beckoned to Tom to come up close, for he could only whisper.

"You've beaten me on the square, and I like you. Don't think I killed my twenty wives. They all died naturally. But call the dogs by name, and they will let you pass. Then, in my vaults, you'll find gold, silver, and copper. Make these your own and bury me decently. This is all I ask."

Tom made himself owner of the castle and all its treasures. He opened the King's Highway again. He took care of his aged mother, married the twenty-first wife of Giant Blubb, now a widow, and was always kind to the sick and poor.

To-day in Cornwall, they still tell stories of the big fellow who abolished Giant Blubb's toll gate.

Centuries afterward, when Christ's gospel came into the land, they restored Giant Tom's tomb and on it were chiseled these words:

THE RESTORER OF PATHS TO DWELL IN.

A Boy that Visited Fairyland

Many are the places in Wales where the ground is lumpy and humpy with tumuli, or little artificial mounds. Among these the sheep graze, the donkeys bray, and the cows chew the cud.

Here the ground is strewn with the ruins of cromlechs, or Cymric strongholds, of old Roman camps, of chapels and monasteries, showing that many different races of men have come and gone, while the birds still fly and the flowers bloom.

Centuries ago, the good monks of St. David had a school where lads were taught Latin and good manners. One of their pupils was a boy named Elidyr. He was such a poor scholar and he so hated books and loved play, that in his case spankings and whippings were almost of daily occurrence. Still he made no improvement. He was in the habit also of playing truant, or what one of the monks called "traveling to Bagdad." One of the consequences was that certain soft parts of his body—apparently provided by nature for this express purpose—often received a warming from his daddy.

His mother loved her boy dearly, and she often gently chided him, but he would not listen to her, and when she urged him to be more diligent, he ran out of the room. The monks did not spare the birch rod, and soon it was a case of a whipping for every lesson not learned.

One day, though he was only twelve years old, the boy started on a long run into the country. The further he got, the happier he felt—at least for one day.

At night, tired out, he crept into a cave. When he woke up, in the morning, he thought it was glorious to be as free as the wild asses. So like them, he quenched his thirst at the brook. But when, towards noon, he could find nothing to eat, and his inside cavity seemed to enlarge with very emptiness, his hunger grew every minute. Then he thought that a bit of oat cake, a leek, or a bowl of oat meal, whether porridge or flummery, might suit a king.

He dared not go out far and pick berries, for, by this time, he saw that people were out searching for him. He did not feel yet, like going back to books, rods and scoldings, but the day seemed as long as a week. Meanwhile, he discovered that he had a stomach, which seemed to grow more and more into an aching void. He was glad when the sunset and darkness came. His bed was no softer in the cave, as he lay down with a stone for his pillow. Yet he had no dreams like those of Jacob and the angels.

When daylight came, the question in his mind was still, whether to stay and starve, or to go home and get two thrashings—one from his daddy, and another from the monks. But how about that thing inside of him, which seemed to be a live creature gnawing away, and which only something to eat would quiet? Finally, he came to a stern resolve. He started out, ready to face two whippings, rather than one death by starvation.

But he did not have to go home yet, for at the cave's mouth, he met two elves, who delivered a most welcome message.

"Come with us to a land full of fun, play, and good things to eat."

All at once, his hunger left him and he forgot that he ever wanted to swallow anything. All fear, or desire to go home, or to risk either schooling or a thrashing, passed away also.

Into a dark passage all three went, but they soon came out into a beautiful country. How the birds sang and the flowers bloomed! All around could be heard the joyful shouts of little folks at play. Never did things look so lovely.

Soon, in front of the broad path along which they were trav-eling, there rose up before him a glorious palace. It had a splen-did gateway, and the silver-topped towers seemed to touch the blue sky.

"What building is this?" asked the lad of his two guides.

They made answer that it was the palace of the King of Fairyland. Then they led him into the throne room, where, sat in golden splendor, a king, of august figure and of majestic presence, who was clad in resplendent robes. He was surrounded by courtiers in rich apparel, and all about him was magnifi-cence, such as this boy, Elidyr, had never even read about or dreamed.

Yet everything was so small that it looked like Toy Land, and he felt like a giant among them, even though many of the little men around him were old enough to have whiskers on their cheeks and beards on their chins.

The King spoke kindly to Elidyr, asking him who he was, and whence he had come.

While talking thus, the Prince, the King's only son ap-peared. He was dressed in white velvet and gold, and had a long feather in his cap. In the pleasantest way, he took Elidyr's hand and said:

"Glad to see you. Come and let us play together."

That was just what Elidyr liked to hear. The King smiled and said to his visitor, "You will attend my son?" Then, with a wave of his hand, he signified to the boys to run out and play games.

A right merry time they did have, for there were many other little fellows for playmates.

These wee folks, with whom Elidyr played, were hardly as big as our babies, and certainly would not reach up to his mother's knee. To them, he looked like a giant, and he richly enjoyed the fun of having such little men, but with beards growing on their faces, look up to him.

They played with golden balls, and rode little horses, with

silver saddles and bridles, but these pretty animals were no larger than small dogs, or grayhounds.

No meat was ever seen on the table, but always plenty of milk. They never told a lie, nor used bad language, or swearwords. They often talked about mortal men, but usually to despise them; because what they liked to do, seemed so absurd and they always wanted foolish and useless things. To the elves, human beings were never satisfied, or long happy, even when they got what they wanted.

Everything in this part of fairyland was lovely, but it was always cloudy. No sun, star or moon was ever seen, yet the little men did not seem to mind it and enjoyed themselves every day. There was no end of play, and that suited Elidyr.

Yet by and by, he got tired even of games and play, and grew very homesick. He wanted to see his mother. So he asked the King to let him visit his old home. He promised solemnly to come back, after a few hours. His Majesty gave his permission, but charged him not to take with him anything whatever from fairyland, and to go with only the clothes on his back.

The same two elves or dwarfs, who had brought him into fairyland, were chosen to conduct him back. When they had led him again through the underground passage into the sunlight, they made him invisible until he arrived at his mother's cottage. She was overjoyed to find that no wolf had torn him to pieces, or wild bull had pushed him over a precipice.

She asked him many questions, and he told her all he had seen, felt, or known.

When he rose up to go, she begged him to stay longer, but he said he must keep his word. Besides, he feared the rod of the monks, or his daddy, if he remained. So he made his mother agree not to tell anything—not even to his father, as to where he was, or what he was doing. Then he made off and reported again to his playmates in fairyland.

The King was so pleased at the lad's promptness in returning, and keeping his word, and telling the truth, that he allowed him to go see his mother as often as he wanted to do so. He even gave orders releasing the two little men from constantly guarding him and told them to let the lad go alone, and when he would, for he always kept his word.

Many times did Elidyr visit his mother. By one road, or another, he made his way, keeping himself invisible all the time, until he got inside her cottage. He ran off, when anyone called in to pay a visit, or when he thought his daddy, or one of the monks was coming. He never saw any of these men.

One day, in telling his mother of the fun and good times he had in fairyland, he spoke of the heavy yellow balls, with which he and the King's sons played, and how these rolled around.

Before leaving home, this boy had never seen any gold, and did not know what it was, but his mother guessed that it was the precious metal, of which the coins called sovereigns, and worth five dollars apiece, were made. So she begged him to bring one of them back to her.

This, Elidyr thought, would not be right; but after much argument, his parents being poor, and she telling him that, out of hundreds in the King's palace, one single ball would not be missed, he decided to please her.

So one day, when he supposed no one was looking, he picked up one of the yellow balls and started off through the narrow dark passageway homeward.

But no sooner was he back on the earth, and in the sunlight again, than he heard footsteps behind him. Then he knew that he had been discovered.

He glanced over his shoulder and there were the two little men, who had led him first and had formerly been his guards. They scowled at him as if they were mad enough to bite off the heads of tenpenny nails. Then they rushed after him, and there began a race to the cottage.

But the boy had legs twice as long as the little men, and got to the cottage door first. He now thought himself safe, but pushing open the door, he stumbled over the copper threshold, and the ball rolled out of his hand, across the floor of hardened clay, even to the nearly white-washed border, which ran about the edges of the room. It stopped at the feet of his mother, whose eyes opened wide at the sight of the ball of shining gold.

As he lay sprawling on the floor, and before he could pick himself up, one of the little men leaped over him, rushed into the room, and, from under his mother's petticoats, picked up the ball.

They spat at the boy and shouted, "traitor," "rascal," "thief," "false mortal," "fox," "rat," "wolf," and other bad names. Then they turned and sped away.

Now Elidyr, though he had been a mischievous boy, often willful, lazy, and never liking his books, had always loved the truth. He was very sad and miserable, beyond the telling, because he had broken his word of honor. So, almost mad with grief and shame, and from an accusing conscience, he went back to find the cave, in which he had slept. He would return to the King of the fairies, and ask his pardon, even if His Majesty never allowed him to visit Fairyland again.

But though he often searched, and spent whole days in trying to find the opening in the hills, he could never discover it.

So, fully penitent, and resolving to live right, and become what his father wanted him to be, he went back to the monastery.

There he plied his tasks so diligently that he excelled all in book-learning. In time, he became one of the most famous scholars in Welsh history. When he died, he asked to be buried, not in the monk's cemetery, but with his father and mother, in the churchyard. He made request that no name, record, or epitaph, be chiseled on his tomb, but only these words:

WE CAN DO NOTHING AGAINST THE TRUTH, BUT ONLY FOR THE TRUTH.

THE WELSHERY AND THE NORMANS

Though their land has been many times invaded, the Welsh have never been conquered. Powerful tribes, like the Romans, Saxons and Normans, have tried to over-whelm them. Even when English and German kings attempted to crush their spirit and blot out their language and literature, the Welsh resisted and won victory.

Among the bullies that tried force, instead of justice, and played the slave-driver, rather than the Good Samaritan's way, were the Normans. These brutal fellows, when they thought that they had overrun Wales with their armies, began to build strong castles all over the country. They kept armed men by the thousands ready, night and day, to rush out and put to death anybody and everybody who had a weapon in his hand. Often they burned whole villages. They killed so many Welsh people that it seemed at times as if they expected to empty the land of its inhabitants. Thus, they hoped to possess all the acres for themselves. They talked as if there were no people so refined and so cultured as they were, while the natives, good and bad, were lumped together as "the Welshery."

Yet all this time, with these hundreds of strong castles, bristling with turrets and towers, no Englishman's life was safe. If he dared to go out alone, even twenty rods from the castle, he was instantly killed by some angry Welshman lying in ambush. So the Normans had to lock themselves up in armor, until they looked like lobsters in their shells. When on their iron-clad horses they resembled turtles, so that if a knight fell off, he had to be chopped open to be rid of his metal clothes.

Yet all this was in vain, for when the Norman marched out in bodies, or rode in squadrons, the Welshery kept away and were hidden.

Even the birds and beasts noticed this, and saw what fools the Normans were, to behave so brutally.

As for the fairies, they met together to see what could be done. Even the reptiles shamed men by living together more peaceably. Only the beasts of prey approved of the Norman way of treating the Welsh people.

At last, it came to pass that, after the long War of the Roses, when the Reds and the Whites had fought together, a Welsh king sat upon the throne of England. Henry VIII was of Cymric ancestry. His full name was Henry Tudor; or, in English, Henry Theodore.

Among the Welsh, every son, to his own name as a child, such as Henry, William, Thomas, etc., added that of his father. Thus it happens that we can usually tell a man by his name; for example, Richards, Roberts, Evans, Jones, etc., etc., that he is a Welshman.

When a Welshman went into England to live, if he were a sister's son, he usually added a syllable showing this, as in the case of Jefferson, which means sister's son. Our great Thomas Jefferson used to boast that he could talk Welsh.

So the living creatures of all sorts in Wales, human beings, fairies, and animals took heart and plucked up courage, when a Tudor king, Henry VIII, sat on the throne.

Now it was Puck who led the fairies as the great peace-maker. He went first to visit all the most ancient creatures, in order to find out who should be offered the post of honor, as ambassador, who should be sent to the great king in London, Henry Tudor, to see what could be done for Wales.

First he called on the male eagle, oldest of all birds. Though not bald-headed, like his American cousin, the Welsh eagle was very old, and at that time a widower. Although he had been father to nine generations of eaglets, he sent Puck to the stag.

This splendid creature, with magnificent antlers, lived at the edge of the forest, near the trunk of an oak tree. It was still standing, but was now a mere shell. Old men said that the children of the aborigines played under it, and here was the home of the god of lightning, which they worshiped.

So to the withered oak, Puck went, and offered him the honor of leadership to an embassy to the King.

But the stag answered and said:

"Well do I remember when an acorn fell from the top of the parent oak. Then, for three hundred years it was growing. Children played under it. They gathered acorns in their aprons, and the archers made bows from its boughs.

Then the oak tree began to die, and, during nearly thirty tens of years it has been fading, and I have seen it all.

Yet there is one older than I. It is the salmon that swims in the Llyn stream. Inquire there."

So of the old mother salmon, Puck went to ask, and this was the answer which he received.

"Count all the spots on my body, and all the eggs in my roe —one for each year. Yet the blackbird is older even than I. Go listen to her story. She excels me, in both talk and fact."

And the blackbird opened its orange-colored bill, and answered proudly:

"Do you see this flinty rock, on which I am sitting? Once it was so huge that three hundred yoke of oxen could hardly move it. Yet, today, it hardly more than affords me room to roost on."

"What made it so small, do you ask?"

"Well, all I have clone to wear it away, has been to wipe my beak on it, every night, before I go to sleep, and in the morning to brush it with the tips of my wing."

Even Puck, fairy though he was, was astonished at this. But the blackbird added:

"Go to the toad, that blinks its eye under the big rock yonder. His age is greater than mine."

The toad was half asleep when Puck came, but it opened with alertness, its beautiful round bright eyes, set in a rim of gold. Then Puck asked the question: "Oh, thou that carriest a jewel in thy head, are there any things alive that are older than thou art?"

"That, I could not be sure of, especially if as many false things are told about them, as are told about me; but when I was a tadpole in the pond, that old hag of an owl was still hooting away, in the treetops, scaring children, as in ages gone. She is older than I. Go and see her. If age makes wise, she is the wisest of all."

Puck went into the forest, but at first saw no bird answering to the description given him.

He said to himself, "She is, I wonder, who?"

He was surprised to hear his question repeated, not as an echo, but by another. Still, he thought it might possibly be his own voice come back.

So, in making a catalogue, in his note book, of what he had seen and heard that day, he put down, "To wit—one echo."

Again came the sound:

"To whit—to who, to whit—to who?" Sounded the voice.

Thinking that this was intended to be a polite question, Puck looked up. Sure enough, there was the wise bird sitting on a bough, above him, as sober as a judge.

"Who! did you ask?" answered Puck and then went on to explain:

"I am Lord of the Fairies in Welshery, and I seek to know which is the most venerable, of all the creatures in the Land of the Red Dragon."

"I am ready to salute you, as the most ancient and honorable of all living things in the Cymric realm. You are desired to bear a message to the Great King, in London."

Tickled by such delicate flattery, and the honors proffered her, this lady owl, after much blinking and winking, flirting, and fluttering, at last agreed to go to King Henry VIII in London. The business, with which she was charged, was to protest against Norman brutality and to plead for justice.

Now this old lady-owl, gray with centuries, though she had such short ears, kept them open by day and during the night, also, for all the gossip that floated in the air. She knew all about everybody and everything. From what she had heard, she expected to find the new King, Henry VIII, a royal fellow in velvet, with a crown on his head, and his body as big and round as a hogshead, sitting in a room full of chopping blocks and battle axes. Further, she fancied she would find a dozen pretty women locked up in his palace, some in the cellar, others in the pantry, and more in the garret; but all waiting to have their heads chopped off.

For the popular story ran that his chief amusement was to marry a wife one day and slice off her head the next.

It was said also that the King kept a private graveyard, and took a walk in it every afternoon to study the epitaphs, which he kept a scholar busy in writing; and also a man, from the marble yard near by, to chisel them on the tombs, after his various wives had been properly beheaded.

But the owl never could find out whether these fables were wicked fibs, or fairy tales, or only street talk.

Puck and the owl together arrived in London, at the palace, when the King was at his dinner. The butlers and lackeys wanted to keep them out, but the merry monarch gave orders to let them in at once. He made the owl perch over the mantel piece, but told Puck to stand upon the dinner table and walk over the tablecloth. The pepper box was put away, so that he should not sneeze and the King carefully removed the mustard pot, for fear the little fairy fellow might fall in it and be drowned in the hot stuff.

His Majesty said that, for the time being, Puck should be the Prince of Wales. Puck strutted about to the amusement of the King and all the Court ladies, but he kept away from the pepper, which made his nose tingle, and from the hot soup, for fear he might tumble into it and be scalded. When the dessert came on, Puck hid himself under a walnut shell, just for fun.

It would take too long to tell about all that was said, or the questions, which the King asked about his Welsh subjects, and which either the owl or the fairy man answered. According to Puck's story, Wales was then a most distressful country, though the Welshery, to a man, wanted to be good and loyal subjects of the Tudors.

Several times did Puck appeal to the owl, to have his story confirmed, because this wise bird had lived among the Cymry, centuries before the Normans came. The owl every time blinked, bowed, and answered solemnly:

"To whit, to who. To whit, to who," which in this case showed that she had learned to speak the Court language.

"Why, bless my soul, the owl speaks good Cockney Hing-lish," whispered one of the butlers, who had been born in Wales.

"Yes, but that is the proper way to address His Majesty, King Ennery the Heighth," answered the other butler, who was a native-born Londoner.

Puck and the owl returned to Wales. What happened after that, is the A B C of history, that everybody knows, and for which all the Welsh people to this day bless the Tudors, who made the Welsh equal before the law with any and all English-men. Even Puck himself had never seen anything like the change that quickly took place for the better, nor did Queen Mab, with her wand, ever work such wonders.

It was better than a fairy tale, and the effects, very soon seen, were even more wonderful. Down went the castles into ruins, for rats to run around in, and wild dogs to yelp and foxes to hide in, or look out of the casements. To-day, what were once ban-queting halls are covered with moss, and on the ground grass grows, over which sheep graze and children play; while rooks and crows nest or roost in the tall towers.

Any Englishman's life was safe anywhere, and Wales be-came one of the most easily governed countries in all the won-derful British Empire.

And in the great world-war, that even children, who read these stories, can remember, Wales, the Land of the Free, the Home of Deathless Democracy, led all the British Isles, colon-ies, islands, or coaling stations around the wide world, in loyalty, valor and sacrifice. And the handsome son of the King, George, the Prince of Wales, led the descendants of Welsh archers, now called the Fusileers. They went into battle, singing, "Old Land our Fathers before us held so dear"; or they marched, following the band that played "The Men of Harlech."

It is because Welsh cherish their traditions, harps, music, language and noble inheritances, with which they feed their souls, that they lead the four nations of the British Isles in the nobler virtues, that keep a nation alive, as well as in the sweet humanities of the Red Cross and in generous hospitality to the refugee Belgian. True to his motto, "I serve," the Prince of Wales who came to see us in 1919—as did his grandfather, whom the story-teller saw when he visited our Independence Hall in 1860—loved to be the servant of his people.

What was it that wrought this peaceful wonder of the six-teenth century? Was it a fairy spell magic ointment, star-tipped wand, treasures of caves, or ocean depths? Was it anything that dragons, giants, ogres, or even swords, spears, catapults, or whips and clubs, or elves or gnomes could do?

Not a bit of it! Only justice and kindness, instead of brutal-ity and force..

THE WELSH FAIRIES HOLD A MEETING

In the ancient Cymric gatherings, the Druids, poets, prophets, seers, and singers all had part. The one most honored as the president of the meeting was crowned and garlanded. Then he was led in honor and sat in the chair of state. They called this great occasion an Eistedfodd, or sitting, after the Cymric word, meaning a chair.

All over the world, the Welsh folks, who do so passionately love music, poetry and their own grand language, hold the Eistedfodd at regular intervals. Thus they renew their love for the Fatherland and what they received long ago from their ancestors.

Now it happens that the fairies in every land usually follow the customs of the mortals among whom they live. The Swiss, the Dutch, the Belgian, the Japanese and Korean fairies, as we all know, although they are much alike in many things are as different from each other as the countries in which they live and play. So, when the Welsh fairies all met together, they resolved to have songs and harp music and make the piper play his tunes just as in the Eistedfodd.

The Cymric fairies of our days have had many troubles to complain of. They were disgusted with so much coal smoke, the poisoning of the air by chemical fumes, and the blackening of the landscape from so many factory chimneys. They had other grievances also.

So the Queen Mab, who had a Welsh name, and another fairy, called Pwca, or in English King Puck, sent out invitations into every part of Wales, for a gathering on the hills, near the great rock called Dina's seat. This is a rocky chair formed by nature. They also included in their call those parts of western and south England, such as are still Welsh and spiritually almost a part of Wales. In fact, Cornwall was the old land, in which the Cymry had first landed when coming from over the sea.

The meeting was to be held on a moonlight night, and far away from any houses, lest the merry making, dancing and singing of the fairies should keep the farmers awake. This was something of which the yokels, or men of the plow, often complained. They could not sleep while the fairies were having their parties.

Now among the Welsh fairies of every sort, size, dress, and behavior, some were good, others were bad, but most of them were only full of fun and mischief. Chief of these was the lively little fellow, Puck, who lived in Cwm Pwcca, that is, Puck Valley, in Breconshire.

Now it had been an old custom, which had come down, from the days of the cave men, that when anyone died, the people, friends and relatives sat up all night with the corpse. The custom arose, at first, with the idea of protection against wild beasts and later from insult by enemies. This was called a wake. The watchers wept and wailed at first, and then fell to eating and drinking. Sometimes, they got to be very lively. The young folks even looked on a wake, after the first hour or two, as fine fun. Strong liquor was too plentiful and it often happened that quarrels broke out. When heads were thus fuddled, men saw or thought they saw, many uncanny things, like leather birds, cave eagles, and the like.

But all these fantastic things and creatures, such as foolish people talk about, and with which they frighten children, such as corpse candles, demons and imps, were ruled out and not invited to the fairy meeting. Some other objects, which ignorant folks believed in, were not to be allowed in the company. The door-keeper was notified not to admit the eagles of darkness, that live in a cave which is never lighted up; or the weird, featherless bird of leather, from the Land of Illusion and Phantasy, that brushes its wing against windows, when a funeral is soon to take place; or the greedy dog with silver eyes. None of these would be permitted to show themselves, even if they came and tried to get in. Some other creatures, not recognized in the good society of Fairyland, were also barred out.

To this gathering, only the bright and lively fairies were welcome. Some of the best natured among the big creatures, and especially giants and dragons, might pay a visit, if they wanted to do so; but all the bad ones, such as lake hags, wraiths, sellers of liquids for wakes, who made men drunk, and all who, under the guise of fairies, were only agents for undertakers, were ruled out. The Night Dogs of the Wicked Hunter Annum, the monster Afang, Cadwallader's Goats, and various, cruel goblins and ogres, living in the ponds, and that pulled cattle down to eat them up, and the immodest mermaids, whose bad behavior was so well known, were crossed off the list of invitations.

No ugly brats, such as wicked fairies were in the habit of putting in the cradles of mortal mothers, when they stole away their babies, were allowed to be present, even if they should come with their mothers. This was to be a perfectly respectable company, and no bawling, squealing, crying, or blubbering was to be permitted.

When they had all gathered together, at the evening hour, there was seen, in the moonlight, the funniest lot of creatures, that one could imagine, but all were neatly dressed and well behaved.

Quite a large number of the famous Fair Family, that moved only in the best society of fairyland, fathers, mothers, cousins, uncles and aunts, were on hand. In fact, some of them had thought it was to be a wake, and were ready for whatever might turn up, whether solemn or frivolous. These were dressed in varied costume.

Queen Mab, who above all else, was a Welsh fairy, and whose name, as everybody knows who talks Cymric, suggested her extreme youth and lively disposition, was present in all her glory.

When they saw her, several learned fairies, who had come from a distance, fell at once into conversation on this subject. One remarked: "How would the Queen like to add another syllable to her name? Then we should call her Mab-gath (which means Kitten, or Little Puss)."

"Well not so bad, however; because many mortal daddies, who have a daughter, call her Puss. It is a term of affection with them and the little girls never seem to be offended."

"Oh! Suppose that in talking to each other we call our Queen Mab-gar, what then?" asked another, with a roguish twinkle in the eye.

"It depends on how you use it," said a wise one dryly. This fairy was a stickler for the correct use of every word. "If you meant 'babyish,' or 'childish,' she, or her friends might demur; but, if you use the term 'love of children,' what better name for a fairy queen?"

"None. There could not be any," they shouted, all at once, "but let us ask our old friend the harper."

Now such a thing as inquiring into each other's ages was not common in Fairy Land. Very few ever asked such a question, for it was not thought to be polite. For, though we hear of ugly fairy brats being put into the cradles, in place of pretty children, no one ever heard, either of fairies being born or of dying, or having clocks, or watches, or looking to see what time it was. Nor did doctors, or the census clerks, or directory people ever trouble the fairy ladies, to ask their age.

Occasionally, however, there was one fairy, so wise, so

learned, and so able to tell what was going to happen to-morrow, or next year, that the other fairies looked up to such an one with respect and awe.

Yet these honorables would hardly know what you were talking about, if you asked any of them how old they might be, or spoke of "old" or "young." If, by any chance, a fairy did use the world "old" in talking of their number, it would be for honor or dignity, and they would mean it for a compliment.

The fact was, that many of the most lively fairies showed their frivolous disposition at once. These were of the kind, that, like kittens, cubs, or babies, wanted to play all the time, yes, every moment. Already, hundreds of them were tripping from flower to flower, riding on the backs of fireflies, or harnessing night moths, or any winged creatures they could saddle, for flight through the air. Or, they were waltzing with glow worms, or playing "ring around a rosy," or dancing in circles. They could not keep still, one moment.

In fact, when a great crowd of the frolicsome creatures got singing together, they made such a noise, that a squad of fairy policemen, dressed in club moss and armed with pistils, was sent to warn them not to raise their voices too high; lest the farmers, especially those that were kind to the fairies, should be awakened, and feel in bad humor.

So the knot of learned fairies had a quiet time to talk, and, when able to hear their own words, the harper, who was very learned, answered their questions about Queen Mab as follows:

"Well, you know the famous children's story book, in which mortals read about us, and which they say they enjoy so much, is named Mabinogion, that is, The Young Folks' Treasury of Cymric Stories."

"It is well named," said another fairy savant, "since Queen Mab is the only fairy that waits on men. She inspires their dreams, when these are born in their brains."

The talk now turned on Puck, who was to be the president of the meeting. They were expected to show much dignity in his presence, but some feared he would, as usual, play his pranks. Before he arrived in his chariot, which was drawn by dragon flies, some of his neighbors that lived in the valley near by chatted about him, until the gossip became quite personal. Just for the fun of it, and the amusement of the crowd, they wanted Puck to give an exhibition, off-hand, of all his very varied accomplishments for he could beat all rivals in his special variety, or as musicians say, his repertoire.

"No. 'Twould be too much like a Merry Andrew's or a Buffoon's sideshow, where the freaks of all sorts are gathered, such as they have at those county fairs, which the mortals get up, to which are gathered great crowds. The charge of admission is a sixpence. I vote 'no.'"

"Well, for the very reason that Puck can beat the rest of us at spells and transformations, I should like to see him do for us as many stunts as he can. I've heard from a mortal, named Shakespeare, that, in one performance, Puck could be a horse, a hound, a hog, a bear without any head, and even kindle himself into a fire; while his vocal powers, as we know, are endless. He can neigh, bark, grunt, roar, and even burn up things. Now, I should like to see the fairy that could beat him at tricks. It was Puck himself, who told the world that he was in the habit of doing all these things, and I want to see whether he was boasting."

"Tut, tut, don't talk that way, about our king," said a fourth fairy.

All this was only chaff and fun, for all the fairies were in good humor. They were only talking, to fill up the interval until the music began.

Now the canny Welsh fairies had learned the trick of catching farthings, pennies and sixpences from the folks who have more curiosity in them than even fairies do. These human beings, cunning fellows that they are, let the curtain fall on a show, just at the most interesting part. Then they tell you to come next day and find out what is to happen. Or, as they say in a story paper, "to be continued in our next."

Or, worse than all, the story teller stops, at some very excit-ing episode, and then passes the hat or collection-box around, to get the copper or silver of his listeners, before he will go on.

This time, however, it was Puck himself who came forward and declared that, unless everyone of the fairies would promise to attend the next meeting, there should be no music. Now a meeting of the Welshery, whether fairies or human, without music was a thing not to be thought of. So, although at first some fairies grumbled and held back, and were quite sulky about it, even muttering other grumpy words, they at last all agreed, and Puck sent for the fiddler to make music for the dance.

KING ARTHUR'S CAVE

In our time, every boy and girl knows about the nuts and blossoms, the twigs and the hedges, the roots and the leaf of the common hazel bush, and everybody has heard of the witch hazel. In old days they made use of the forked branches of the hazel as a divining rod. With this, they believed that they could divine, or find out the presence of treasures of gold and silver, deep down in the earth, and hidden from human eyes.

And, what boy or girl has never played the game, and sung the ditty, "London Bridge is falling down, falling down, falling down," even though nobody now living ever saw it fall?

Now, our story is about a hazel rod, a Welshman on London Bridge, treasures in a cave, and what happened because of these.

It was in the days when London Bridge was not, as we see it to-day, a massive structure of stone and iron, able to bear up hundreds of cars, wagons, horses and people, and lighted at night with electric bulbs. No, when this Welshman visited London, the bridge had a line of shops on both sides of the passage way, and reaching from end to end.

Taffy was the name of this fellow from Denbigh, in Wales, and he was a drover. He had brought, all the way from one of the richest of the Welsh provinces, a great drove of Black Welsh cattle, such as were in steady demand by Englishmen, who have always been lovers of roast beef. Escaping all the risks of cattle thieves, rustlers, and highwaymen, he had sold his beeves at a good price; so that his pockets were now fairly bulging out with gold coins, and yet this fellow wanted more. But first, before going home, he would see the sights of the great city, which then contained about a hundred thousand people.

While he was handling some things in a shop, to decide what he should take home to his wife, his three daughters and his two little boys, he noticed a man looking intently, not at him, but at his stick. After a while, the stranger came up to him and asked him where he came from.

Now Taffy was not very refined in his manners, and he thought it none of the fellow's business. He was very surly and made reply in a gruff voice.

"I come from my own country."

The stranger did not get angry, but in a polite tone made answer:

"Don't be offended at my question. Tell me where you cut that hazel stick, and I'll make it to your advantage, if you will take my advice."

Even yet Taffy was gruff and suspicious.

"What business is it of yours, where I cut my hazel stick?" he answered.

"Well it may matter a good deal to you, if you will tell me. For, if you remember the place, and can lead me to it, I'll make you a rich man, for near that spot lies a great treasure."

Taffy was not much of a thinker, apart from matters concerning cattle, and his brain worked slowly! He was sorely puzzled. Here was a wizard, who could make him rich, and he did so love to jingle gold in his pockets. But then he was superstitious. He feared that this sorcerer derived all his uncanny knowledge from demons, and Taffy, being rather much of a sinner, feared these very much. Meanwhile, his new acquaintance kept on persuading him.

Finally Taffy yielded and the two went on together to Wales.

Now in this country, there are many stones placed in position, showing they were not there by accident, but were reared by men, to mark some old battle, or famous event. And for this, rough stone work, no country, unless it be Korea or China, is more famous than Wales.

On reaching one called the Fortress Rock, Taffy pointed to an old hazel root, and said to his companion:

"There! From that stock, I cut my hazel stick. I am sure of it."

The sorcerer looked at Taffy to read his face, and to be certain that he was telling the truth. Then he said:

"Bring shovels and we'll both dig."

These having been brought, the two began to work until the perspiration stood out in drops on their foreheads. First the sod and rooty stuff, and then down around the gravelly mass below, they plied their digging tools. Taffy was not used to such toil, and his muscles were soon weary. But, urged on by visions of gold, he kept bravely at his task.

At last, when ready to drop from fatigue, he heard his companion say:

"We've struck it!"

A few shovelfuls more laid bare a broad flat stone. This they pried up, but it required all their strength to lift and stand it on edge. Just below, they saw a flight of steps. They were slippery with wet and they looked very old, as if worn, ages ago, by many feet passing up and down them.

Taffy shrunk back, as a draught of the close, dead air struck his nostrils.

"Come on, and don't be afraid. I'm going to make you rich," said the sorcerer.

At this, Taffy's eyes glistened, and he followed on down the steps, without saying a word. At the bottom of the descent, they entered a narrow passage, and finally came to a door.

"Now, I'll ask you. Are you brave, and will you come in with me, if I open this door?"

By this time, Taffy was so eager for treasure, that he spoke up at once.

"I'm not afraid. Open the door."

The sorcerer gave a jerk and the door flew open. What a sight!

There, in the faint, red light, Taffy discerned a great cave. Lying on the floor were hundreds of armed men, but motionless and apparently sound asleep. Little spangles of light were reflected from swords, spears, round shields, and burnished helmets. All these seemed of very ancient pattern. But immediately in front of them was a bell. Taffy felt some curiosity to tap it. Would the sleeping host of men then rise up?

Just then, the sorcerer, speaking with a menacing gesture, and in a harsh tone, said:

"Do not touch that bell, or it's all up with us both."

Moving carefully, so as not to trip, or to stumble over the sleeping soldiers, they went on, and Taffy, stopping and looking up beheld before him a great round table. Many warriors were sitting at it. Their splendid gold inlaid armor, glittering helmets and noble faces showed that they were no common men. Yet Taffy could see only a few of the faces, for all had their heads more or less bent down, as if sound asleep, though sword and spear were near at hand, ready to be grasped in a moment.

Outshining all, was a golden throne at the farther end of the table and on it sat a king. He was of imposing stature, and august presence. Upon his head was a crown, on which were inlaid or set precious stones. These shone by their own light, sending out rays so brilliant that they dazzled Taffy, who had never seen anything like them. The king held in his right hand a mighty sword. It had a history and the name of it was Excalibur. In Arthur's hand, it was almost part of his own soul. Its hilt and handle were of finely chased gold, richly studded with gems. Yet his head, too, was bent in deep sleep, as if only thunder could wake him.

"Are they all, everyone, asleep?" asked Taffy.

"Each and all," was the answer.

"When did they fall asleep?" asked the drover.

"Over a thousand years ago," answered the sorcerer.

"Tell me who they are, and why here," asked Taffy.

"They are King Arthur's trusty warriors. They are waiting for the hour to come, when they shall rise up and destroy the enemies of the Cymry, and once again possess the whole island of Britain, as in the early ages, before the Saxons came."

"And who are those sitting around the table?" asked Taffy.

The sorcerer seemed tired of answering questions, but he replied, giving the name of each knight, and also that of his father, as if he were a Welshman himself; but at this, Taffy grew impatient, feeling as if a book of genealogy had been hurled at him.

Most impolitely, he interrupted his companion and cried out:

"And who is that on the throne?"

The sorcerer looked as if he was vexed, and felt insulted, but he answered:

"It's King Arthur himself, with Excalibur, his famous sword, in his hand."

This was snapped out, as if the sorcerer was disgusted at the interruption of his genealogy, and he shut his mouth tight as if he would answer no more questions, for such an impolite fellow.

Seizing Taffy by the hand, he led him into what was the storehouse of the cave. There lay heaps upon heaps of yellow gold. Both men stuffed their pockets, belt bags, and the inside of their clothes, with all they could load in.

"Now we had better get out, for it is time to go," said the sorcerer and he led the way towards the cave door.

But as Taffy passed back, and along the hall, where the host of warriors were sleeping, his curiosity got the better of him.

He said to himself, "I must see this host awake. I'll touch that bell, and find out whether the sorcerer spoke the truth."

So, when he came to it, he struck the bell. In the twinkling of an eye, thousands of warriors sprang up, seized their armor, girded their swords, or seized their spears. All seemed eagerly awaiting the command to rush against the foe.

The ground quaked with their tramping, and shook with their tread, until Taffy thought the cave roof would fall in and bury them all. The air resounded with the rattle of arms, as the men, when in ranks, marked time, ready for motion forward and out of the cave.

But from the midst of the host, a deep sounding voice, as earnest as if in hot temper, but as deliberate as if in caution against a false alarm, spoke. He inquired:

"Who rang that bell? Has the day come?"

The sorcerer, thoroughly frightened and trembling, answered:

"No, the day has not come. Sleep on."

Taffy, though dazzled by the increasing brilliancy of the light, had heard another deep voice, more commanding in its tones than even a king's, call out, "Arthur, awake, the bell has rung. The day is breaking. Awake, great King Arthur!"

But even against such a voice, that of the sorcerer, now scared beyond measure, lest the king and his host should discover the cheat, and with his sword, Excalibur, chop the heads off both Taffy and himself, answered:

"No, it is still night. Sleep on, Arthur the Great."

Erect over all, his head aloft and crowned with jewels, as with stars, the King himself now spoke:

"No, my warriors, the day has not yet come, when the Black Eagle and the Golden Eagle will meet in war. Sleep on, loyal souls. The morning of Wales has not yet dawned."

Then, like the gentle soughing of the evening breeze among forest trees, all sound died away, and in the snap of a finger, all were asleep again. Seizing the hand of Taffy, the sorcerer hurried him out of the cave, moved the stone back in its place and motioning to Taffy to do the same, he quickly shoveled and kicked the loose dirt in the hole and stamped it down: When Taffy turned to look for him, he was gone, without even taking the trouble to call his dupe a fool.

Wearied with his unwonted labors and excitements, Taffy walked home, got his supper, pondered on what he had seen, slept, and awoke in the morning refreshed. After breakfast, he sallied out again with pick and shovel.

For months, Taffy dug over every square foot of the hill. Neglecting his business as cattle man, he spent all the money he had made in London, but he never found that entrance to the cave. He died a poor man and all his children had to work hard to get their bread.

THE LADY OF THE LAKE

One easily gets acquainted with the Welsh fairies, for nearly all the good ones are very fond of music.

Or, they live down in the lakes, or up in the mountains. They are always ready to help kind or polite people, who treat them well or will give them a glass of milk, or a saucer of flummery.

But, oh, what tricks and mischief they do play on mean or stingy or grumpy folks with bad tempers! They tangle up the harness of the horses; milk the cows, letting the milk go to waste, on the stable floor; tie knots in their tails, or keep the dog's mouth shut, when the robbers come sneaking around. Better not offend a fairy, even though no higher than a thimble!

A favorite place for the elfin ladies of the lake is high up in one of the fresh water mountain ponds. They are cousins to the mermaids, that swim in the salt water.

They say that these lake maidens love to come up close to the shore, to smell the sweet grass and flowers, which the cows like so much.

Near one of these lakes dwelt a widow, with only one son, named Gwyn. One day he took his lunch of barley bread and cheese, and went out, as usual, to tend the cows. Soon he saw rising out of the water, to dress her long and luxuriant hair, the most beautiful lady he had ever seen. In her hand she held a golden comb, and was using the bright lake-surface as a mirror.

At once Gwyn fell in love with her, and, like an unselfish lad, held out his refreshments—barley bread and cheese—all he had —bidding her to come and take.

But though the lady glided toward him, while he still held out his hand, she shook her head, saying:

> O thou of the hard baked bread,
> It is not easy to catch me

Sorry enough to miss such a prize, he hurried home to tell his mother. She, wondering also, whether fairies have teeth to chew, told him to take soft dough next time. Then, perhaps, the strange lady would come again.

Not much sleep did the boy get that night, and, before the sun was up, he was down by the lake side holding out his dough.

There, hour after hour, neglecting the cows, he looked eagerly over the water, but nothing appeared, except ripples started by the breeze. Again and again, he gazed in hope, only to be disappointed.

Meanwhile he thought out a pretty speech to make to her, but he kept his dough and went hungry.

It was late in the afternoon, when the trees on the hills were casting long shadows westward, that he gave up watching, for he supposed she would come no more.

But just as he started to go back to his mother's cabin, he turned his head and there was the same lady, looking more beautiful than ever. In a moment, he forgot every word he meant to say to her. His tongue seemed to leave him, and he only held out his hand, with the dough in it.

But the lake lady, shaking her head, only laughed and said:

> Thou of the soft bread
> I will not have thee

Though she dived under the water and left him sad and lonely, she smiled so sweetly, as she vanished, that, though again disap -

pointed, he thought she would come again and she might yet accept his gift.

His mother told him to try her with bread half baked, that is, midway between hard crust and soft dough.

So, having packed his lunch, and much excited, though this time with bright hopes, Gwyn went to bed, though not to sleep. At dawn, he was up again and out by the lake side, with his half baked bread in his hand.

It was a day of rain and shine, of sun burst and cloud, but no lady appeared.

The long hours, of watching and waiting, sped on, until it was nearly dark.

When just about to turn homewards, to ease his mother's anxiety, what should he see, but some cows walking on the surface of the water! In a few minutes, the lady herself, lovelier than ever, rose up and moved towards the shore.

Gwyn rushed out to meet her, with beseeching looks and holding the half baked bread in his hand. This time, she graciously took the gift, placed her other hand in his, and he led her to the shore.

Standing with her on land, he could not speak for many seconds. He noticed that she had sandals on her feet, and the one on the right foot was tied in a way rather unusual. Under her winsome smile, at last, he regained the use of his tongue. Then he burst out:

"Lady I love you, more than all the world besides. Will you be my wife?"

She did not seem at all willing at first, but love begets love. Finally yielding to his pleadings, she said, rather solemnly:

"I will be your bride but only on this condition, that if you strike me three times, without cause, I will leave your house and you only will be to blame, and it will be forever."

These words stuck in his mind, and he inwardly made a vow never to give his lovely wife cause to leave him.

But not yet did happiness come, for, even while he took oath that he would rather cut off his right hand, than offend her, she darted away like an arrow, and, diving in the lake, disappeared.

At this sudden blow to his hopes and joy, Gwyn was so sorely depressed, as to wish to take his own life. Rushing up to the top of a rock, overhanging the deepest part of the lake, he was just about to leap into the water and drown himself, when he heard a voice behind him, saying:

"Hold rash lad, come here!"

He looked and there down on the shore of the lake, stood a grand looking old man, with a long white beard. On either side of him was a lovely maiden. These were his daughters.

Trembling with fear, the lad slipped down from the rock and drew near. Then the old man spoke comfortably to him, though in a very cracked voice.

"Mortal, do you wish to marry one of my daughters? Show me the one you love more than the other, and I will consent."

Now the two maidens were so beautiful, yet so exactly alike, that Gwyn could not note any difference. As he looked, he began to wonder whether it had been a different lady, in each case, that rose out of the water. He looked beyond the old man, to see if there were a third lady. When he saw none more, he became more distracted. He feared lest he might choose the wrong one, who had not promised to love him.

Almost in despair, he was about to run home, when he noticed that one of the maidens put forward her right foot. Then he saw that her sandal was tied in the way he had already wondered at. So he boldly went forward and took her by the hand.

"This one is mine," said he to the father.

"You are right," answered the old man. "This is my daughter Nelferch. Take her and you shall have as many cattle, sheep, horses, hogs, and goats, as she can count, of each, without drawing in her breath. But I warn you that three blows, without cause, will send her back to me."

While the old man smiled, and Gwyn renewed his vow, the

new wife began to count by fives—one, two, three, four, five.

At the end of each count drawing in a fresh breath, there rose up, out of the lake, as many sheep, cattle, goats, pigs, and horses, as she had counted.

So it happened that the lad, who went out of his mother's cottage, in the morning, a poor boy, came back to her, a rich man, and leading by the hand the loveliest creature on whom man or woman had ever looked upon.

As for the old man and the other daughter, no one ever saw them again.

Gwyn and his wife went out to a farm which he bought, and oh, how happy they were! She was very kind to the poor. She had the gift of healing, knew all the herbs, which were good for medicine, and cured sick folk of their diseases.

Three times the cradle was filled, and each time with a baby boy. Eight long and happy years followed. They loved each other so dearly and were so happy together, that Gwyn's vow passed entirely out of his mind, and he thought no more of it.

On the seventh birthday of the oldest boy, there was a wedding at some distance away, and the father and mother walked through a field where their horses were grazing. As it was too far for Lady Nelferch to walk all the way, her husband went back to the house, for saddle and bridle, while she should catch the horse.

"Please do, and bring me my gloves from off the table," she called, as he turned towards the house.

But when he returned to the field, he saw that she had not stirred. So, before handing his wife her gloves and pointing playfully to the horses, he gave her a little flick with the gloves.

Instead of moving, instantly, she heaved a deep sigh. Then looking up at him with sorrowful and reproachful eyes, she said:

"Remember our vow, Gwyn. This is the first causeless blow. May there never be another."

Days and years passed away so happily, that the husband and father never again had to recall the promise given to his wife and her father.

But when they were invited to the christening of a baby, every one was full of smiles and gayety, except Nelferch. Women, especially the older ones, often cry at a wedding, but why his wife should burst into tears puzzled Gwyn.

Tapping her on the shoulder, he asked the reason:

"Because," said she, "this weak babe will be in pain and misery all its days and die in agony. And, husband dear, you have once again struck me a causeless blow. Oh, do be on your guard, and not again break your promise."

From this time forth, Gwyn was on watch over himself, day and night, like a sentinel over whom hangs the sentence of death, should he fall asleep on duty. He was ever vigilant lest, he, in a moment of forgetfulness, might, by some slip of conduct, or in a moment of forgetfulness, strike his dear wife.

The baby, whose life of pain and death of agony Nelferch had foretold, soon passed away; for, happily, its life was short. Then she and her husband attended the last rites of sorrow, for Celtic folk always have a funeral and hold a wake, even when a baby, only a span long, lies in the coffin.

Yet in the most solemn moment of the services of burial, Nelferch the wife, laughed out, so long and with such merriment, that everyone was startled.

Her husband, mortified at such improper behavior, touched her gently, saying:

"Hush, wife! Why do you laugh?"

"Because the babe is free from all pain. And, you have thrice struck me! Farewell!"

Fleeing like a deer home to their farm, she called together, by its name, each and every one of their animals, from stable and field; yes, even those harnessed to the plow. Then, over the mountain all moved in procession to the lake.

There, they plunged in and vanished. No trace of them was left, except that made by the oxen drawing the plow, and which mark on the ground men still point out.

Broken hearted and mad with grief, **Gwyn** rushed into the lake and was seen no more. The three sons, grieving over their drowned father, spent their many days wandering along the lakeside, hoping once more to see one, or both, of their dear parents.

Their love was rewarded. They never saw their father again, but one day their mother, Nelferch, suddenly appeared out of the water. Telling her children that her mission on earth was to relieve pain and misery, she took them to a point in the lake, where many plants grew that were useful in medicine. There, she often came and taught them the virtues of the roots, leaves, juices and the various virtues of the herbs, and how to nurse the sick and heal those who had diseases.

All three of Nelferch's sons became physicians of fame and power. Their descendants, during many centuries, were renowned for their skill in easing pain and saving life. To this day, Physicians' Point is shown to visitors as a famous spot, and in tradition is almost holy.

THE KING'S FOOT HOLDER

There was a curious custom in the far olden times of Wales. At the banqueting hall, the king of the country would sit with his feet in the lap of a high officer.

Whenever His Majesty sat down to dinner, this official person would be under the table holding the royal feet. This was also the case while all sat around the evening fire in the middle of the hall. This footholding person was one of the king's staff and every castle must have a human footstool as part of its furniture.

By and by, it became the fashion for pretty maidens to seek this task, or to be chosen for the office. Their names in English sounded like Foot-Ease, Orthopede, or Foot Lights. When she was a plump and petite maid, they nicknamed her Twelve Inches, or when unusually soothing in her caresses of the soft royal toes. It was considered a high honor to be the King's Foot Holder. In after centuries, it was often boasted of that such and such an ancestor had held this honorable service.

One picture of castle life, as given in one of the old books tells how Kaim, the king's officer, went to the mead cellar with a golden cup, to get a drink that would keep them all wide awake. He also brought a handful of skewers on which they were to broil the collops, or bits of meat at the fire.

While they were doing this, the King sat on a seat of green rushes, over which was spread a flame-colored satin cover, with a cushion like it, for his elbow to rest upon.

In the evening, the harpers and singers made music, the bards recited poetry, or the good story tellers told tales of heroes and wonders. During all this time, one or more maidens held the king's feet, or took turns at it, when tired; for often the revels or songs and tales lasted far into the night. At intervals, if the story was dull, or he had either too much dinner, or had been out hunting and got tired, His Majesty took a nap, with his feet resting upon the lap of a pretty maiden. This happened often in the late hours, while they were getting the liquid refreshments ready.

Then the king's chamberlain gently nudged him, to be wideawake, and he again enjoyed the music, and the stories, while his feet were held.

For, altogether, it was great fun.

Now there was once a Prince of Gwynedd, in Wales, named Math, who was so fond of having his feet held, that he neglected to govern his people properly. He spent all his time lounging in an easy chair, while a pretty maiden held his heels and toes. He committed all public cares to two of his nephews. These were named for short, Gily and Gwyd.

The one whom the king loved best to have her hold his feet was the fairest maiden in all the land, and she was named Goewen.

By and by, the prince grew so fond of having his feet held, and stroked and patted and played with, by Goewen, that he declared that he could not live, unless Goewen held his feet. And, she said, that if she did not hold the king's feet, she would die.

Now this Gily, one of the king's nephews, son of Don, whom he had appointed to look day by day after public affairs, would often be in the hall at night. He listened to the music and stories, and seeing Goewen, the king's foot holder, he fell in love with her. His eye usually wandered from the story teller to the lovely girl holding the king's feet, and he thought her as beautiful as an angel.

Soon he became so lovesick, that he felt he would risk or

give his life to get and have her for his own. But what would the king say?

Besides, he soon found out that the maiden Goewen cared nothing for him.

Nevertheless the passion of the love-lorn youth burned hotly and kept increasing. He confided his secret to his brother Gwyd, and asked his aid, which was promised. So, one day, the brother went to King Math, and begged for leave to go to Pryderi. In the king's name, he would ask from him the gift of a herd of swine of famous breed; which, in the quality of the pork they furnished, excelled all other pigs known. They were finer than any seen in the land, or ever heard of before. Their flesh was said to be sweeter, juicier, and more tender than the best beef. Even their manners were better than those of some men.

In fact, these famous pigs were a present from the King of Fairyland. So highly were they prized, that King Math doubted much whether his nephew could get them at any price.

In ancient Wales the bards and poet singers were welcomed, and trusted above all men; and this, whether in the palace or the cottage.

So Gwyd, the brother of the love-sick one, in order to get the herd of surpassing swine, took ten companions, all young men and strong, dressed as bards, and pretending by their actions to be such. Then they all started out together to seek the palace of Pryderi.

Having arrived, they were entertained at a great feast, in the castle hall. There Pryderi sat on his throne-chair, with his feet in a maiden's lap.

The dinner over, Gwyd was asked to tell a story.

This he did, delighting everyone so much, that he was voted a jolly good fellow by all. In fact, Pryderi felt ready to give him anything he might demand, excepting always his foot holder.

At once, Gwyd made request to give him the herd of swine.

At this, the countenance of Pryderi fell, for he had made a promise to his people, that he would not sell or give away the swine, until they had produced double their number in the land; for there were no pigs and no pork like theirs, to be bought anywhere.

Now this Gwyd was not very cunning, but he had the power of using magic arts. By these, he could draw the veil of illusion over both the mind and the eyes of the people.

So he made answer to Pryderi's objections thus:

"Keep your promise to your people, oh, most honored Pryderi, and only exchange them for the gift I make thee," said Gwyd.

Thereupon, exerting his powers of magic, he created the illusion of twelve superb horses. These were all saddled, bridled, and magnificently caparisoned. But, after twenty-four hours, they would vanish from sight. The illusion would be over.

With these steeds, so well fitted for hunting, were twelve sleek, fleet hounds. Taken altogether, here was a sight to make a hunter's eyes dance with delight.

So Pryderi gave Gwyd the swine, and he quickly drove them off.

"For," he whispered to his companion fellows in knavery, "the illusion will only last until the same hour to-morrow."

And so it happened. For when Pryderi's men went to the stables, to groom the horses and feed the hounds, there was nothing in either the stables or the kennels.

When they told this to Pryderi, he at once blew his horn and assembled his knights, to invade the country of Gwynedd, to recover his swine. Hearing of his coming, King Math went out to meet Pryderi in battle.

But while he was away with his army, Gily, the lover, seized the beautiful maiden Goewen, who held the king's feet in her lap.

She was not willing to marry Gily, but he eloped with her, and carried her off to his cottage.

The war which now raged was finally decided by single combat, as was the custom in old days. By this, the burning of the peasants' houses, and the ruin which threatened the whole country, ended, and peace came.

It was not alone by the strength and fierceness of King Math, but also by the magic spells of Gwyd, that Pryderi was slain.

After burying the hero, King Math came back to his palace and found out what Gily had done. Then he took Goewen away from Gily, and to make amends for her trouble, in being thus torn from his palace, King Math made her his queen. Then the lovely Goewen shared his throne covered with the flame colored satin. One of the most beautiful maidens of the court was chosen to hold his feet, until such time as a permanent choice was made.

As for the two nephews, who had fled from the wrath of their princely uncle, they were put under bans, as outlaws, and had to live on the borders of the kingdoms. No one of the king's people was allowed to give them food or drink. Yet they would not obey the summons of the king, to come and receive their punishment.

But at last, tired of being deserted by all good men and women, they repented in sorrow. Hungry, ragged and forlorn, they came to their uncle, the king to submit themselves to be punished.

When they appeared, Math spoke roughly to them, and said:

"You cannot make amends for the shame you have brought upon me. Yet, since you obey and are sorry, I shall punish you for a time and then pardon you. You are to do penance for three years at least."

Then they were changed into wild deer, and he told them to come back after twelve months.

At the end of the year they returned, bringing with them a young fawn.

As this creature was entirely innocent, it was given a human form and baptized in the church.

But the two brothers were changed into wild swine, and driven off to find their food in the forest.

At the end of the year, they came back with a young pig.

The king had the little animal changed into a human being, which, like every mother's child in that time, received baptism.

Again the brothers were transformed into animal shape. This time, as wolves, and were driven out to the hills.

At the end of a twelve months' period, they came back, three in number, for one was a cub.

By this time, the penance of the naughty nephews was over, and they were now to be delivered from all magic spells.

So their human nature was restored to them, but they must be washed thoroughly. In the first place, it took much hot water and lye, made from the wood ashes, and then a great deal of scrubbing, to make them presentable.

Then they were anointed with sweet smelling oil, and the king ordered them to be arrayed in elegant apparel. They were appointed to hold honorable office at court, and from time to time to go out through the country, to call the officers to attend to public business.

When the time came that the king sought for one of the most beautiful maidens, who should hold his feet, Gwyd nominated to the prince's notice his sister Arianrod. The king was gracious, and thereafter she held his feet at all the banquets. She was looked up to with reverence by all, and held the office for many years. Thus King Math's reputation for grace and mercy was confirmed.

POWELL, PRINCE OF DYFED

One of the oldest of the Welsh fairy tales tells us about Pwyle, King of Fairyland and father of the numerous clan of the Powells. He was a mighty hunter. He could ride a horse, draw a bow, and speak the truth. He was always honored by men, and he kept his faith and his promises to women. The children loved him, for he loved them. In the castle hall, he could tell the best stories. No man, bard, or warrior, foot holder or commoner, could excel him in gaining and keeping the attention of his hearers, even when they were sleepy and wanted to go to bed.

One day, when out a hunting in the woods, he noticed a pack of hounds running down a stag. He saw at once that they were not his own, for they were snow white in color and had red ears.

Being a young man, Powell did not know at this time of his life, that red is the fairy color, and that these were all dogs from Fairyland. So he drove off the red-eared hounds, and was about to let loose his own pack on the stag, when a horseman appeared on the scene.

The stranger at once began to upbraid Powell for being impolite. He asked why his hounds should not be allowed to hunt the deer.

Powell spoke pleasantly in reply, making his proper excuses to the horseman. The two began to like each other, and soon got acquainted and mutually enjoyed being companions.

It turned out that the stranger was Arawn, a king in Fairy-land. He had a rival named Hargan, who was beating him and his army in war.

So Arawn asked Powell to help him against his enemy. He even made request that one year from that time, Powell should meet Hargan in battle. He told him that one stroke of his sword would finish the enemy. He must then sheathe his weapon, and not, on any account, strike a second time.

To make victory sure, the Fairy King would exchange shapes with the mortal ruler and each take not only the place, but each the shape and form of the other. Powell must go into Fairy Land and govern the kingdom there, while Arawn should take charge of affairs at Dyfed.

But Powell was warned, again, to smite down his enemy with a single stroke of his sword. If, in the heat of the conflict, and the joy of victory, Powell should forget, and give a second blow to Hargan, he would immediately come to life and be as strong as ever.

Powell heeded well these words. Then, putting on the shape of Arawn, he went into Fairy Land, and no one noticed, or thought of anything different from the days and years gone by.

But now, at night, a new and unexpected difficulty arose. Arawn's beautiful wife was evidently not in the secret, for she greeted Powell as her own husband.

After dinner, when the telling of stories in the banqueting hall was over, the time had come for them to retire.

But the new bed fellow did not even kiss her, or say "good night," but turned his back to her and his face to the wall, and never moved until daylight. Then the new King in Fairy Land rose up, ate his breakfast, and went out to hunt.

Every day, he ruled the castle and kingdom, as if he had always been the monarch. To everybody, he seemed as if he had been long used to public business, and no questions were asked, nor was there any talk made on the subject. Everyone took things as matter of course.

Yet, however polite or gracious he might be to the queen during the day, in the evening, he spoke not a word, and passed every night as at the first.

The twelve months soon sped along, and now the time for the battle in single combat between Powell and Hargan had fully come. The two warriors met in the middle of a river ford, and backed their horses for a charge. Then they rushed furiously at the other. Powell's spear struck Hargan so hard, that he was knocked out of the saddle and hurled, the length of a lance, over and beyond the crupper, or tail strap of his horse. He fell mortally wounded upon the ground.

Now came the moment of danger and temptation to Powell, for Hargan cried out:

"For the love of Heaven, finish your work on me. Slay me with your sword."

But Powell was wise and his head was cool. He had kept in mind the warning to strike only one blow. He called out loudly, so that all could hear him:

"I will not repeat that. Slay thee who may, I shall not."

So Hargan, knowing his end had come, bade his nobles bear him away from the river shore.

Then Powell, with his armies, overran the two kingdoms of Fairy Land and made himself master of all. He took oath of all the princes and nobles, who swore to be loyal to their new master.

This done, Powell rode away to the trysting place in a glen, and there he met Arawn, as had been appointed. They changed shapes, and each became himself, as he had been before.

Arawn thanked Powell heartily, and bade him see what he had done for him.

Then each one rode back, in his former likeness, to his kingdom.

Now at Anwyn, no one but Arawn himself knew that anything unusual had taken place. After dinner, and the evening story telling were over, and it was time to go to bed, Arawn's wife was surprised in double measure.

Two things puzzled her. Her husband was now very tender to her and also very talkative; whereas, for a whole year, every night, he had been as silent and immovable as a log. How could it be, in either case?

But this time, the wife was silent as a statue. Even though Arawn spoke to her three times, he received no reply.

Then he asked directly of her, why she was so silent. She made an answer that, for a whole year, no word had been spoken in their bedroom.

"What?" said he, "did we not talk together, as always before?"

"No," said she, "not for a year has there been talk or caress between us."

At this answer, Arawn was overcome with surprise, and as struck with admiration at having so good a friend. He burst out first in praise of Powell, and then told his wife all that had happened during the past twelve months. She, too, was full of admiration, and told her husband that in Powell he had certainly found a true friend.

In Dyfed, when Powell had returned to his own land and castle, he called his lords together. Then he asked them to be perfectly frank and free to speak. They must tell him whether they thought him a good king during the year past.

All shouted in chorus of approval. Then their spokesman addressed Powell thus:

"My lord, never was thy wisdom so great, thy generosity more free, nor thy justice more manifest, than during the past year."

When he ceased, all the vassals showed their approval of this speech.

Then Powell, smiling, told the story of his adventures in exchanging his form and tasks; at the end of which, the spokesman taking his cue from the happy faces of all his fellow vassals, made reply:

"Of a truth, lord, we pray thee, do thou give thanks to Heaven that thou hast formed such a fellowship. Please continue to us the form of the kingdom and rule, that we have enjoyed for a year past."

Thereupon King Powell took oath, kissing the hilt of his sword, and called on Heaven to witness his promise that he would do as they had desired.

So the two kings confirmed the friendship they had made. Each sent the other rich gifts of jewels, horses and hounds.

In memory of so wonderful and happy union, of a mortal and a fairy, Powell was thereafter, in addition to all his titles, saluted as Lord of Anwyn, which is only another name for the Land of the Fairies.

POWELL AND HIS BRIDE

Not far from the castle where King Powell had his court, there was a hillock called the Mount of Macbeth. It was the common belief that some strange adventure would befall anyone who should sit upon that mound.

He would receive blows, or wounds, or else he would see something wonderful.

Thus it came to pass, that none but peaceful bards had ever sat upon the mound. Never a warrior or a common man had risked sitting there. The general fear felt, and the awe inspired by the place, was too great.

But after his adventure of being King of Fairy Land for a whole year, everything else to Powell seemed dull and commonplace. So, to test his own courage, and worthiness of kingship, Powell assembled all his lords at Narberth.

After the night's feasting, revelry and story telling, Powell declared that, next day, he would sit upon the enchanted mound.

So when the sun was fully risen, Powell took his seat upon the mound, expecting that, all of a sudden, something unusual would happen.

For some minutes nothing, whether event or vision, took place. Then he lifted up his eyes and saw approaching him a white horse on which rode a lady. She was dressed in shining garments, as if made of gold. Evidently she was a princess. Yet she came not very near.

"Does anyone among you know who this lady is?" asked Powell of his chieftains.

"Not one of us," was the answer.

Thereupon Powell ordered his vassals to ride forward. They were to greet her courteously, and inquire who she was.

But now the predicted wonder took place. She moved away from them, yet at a quiet pace that suited her. Though the knights spurred their horses, and rode fast and furiously, they could not come any nearer to her.

They galloped back, and reported their failure to reach the lady.

Then Powell picked out others and sent them riding after the lady, but each time, one and all returned, chagrined with failure. A woman had beaten them.

So the day closed with silence in the castle hall. There was no merry making or story telling that night.

The next day, Powell sat again on the mound and once more the golden lady came near.

This time, Powell himself left his seat on the mound, leaped on his fleetest horse, and pursued the maiden, robed in gold, on the white horse.

But she flitted away, as she had done before from the knights. Again and again, though he could get nearer and nearer to her, he failed.

Then the baffled king cried out, in despair, "O maiden fair, for the sake of him whom thou lovest, stay for me."

Evidently the lady, who lived in the time of castles and courts, did not care to be wooed in the style of the cave men. Such manners did not suit her, but with a change of method of making love, her heart melted. Besides, she was a kind woman. She took pity on horses, as well as on men.

Sweet was her voice, as she answered most graciously:

"I will stay gladly, and it were better for thy horses, hadst thou asked me properly, long ago."

To his questions, as to how and why she came to him, she

told her story, as follows:

"I am Rhiannon, descended from the August and Venerable One of old. My aunts and uncles tried to make me marry against my will a chieftain named Gwawl, an auburn-haired youth, son of Clud, but, because of my love to thee, would I have no husband, and if you reject me, I will never marry any man."

"As Heaven is my witness, were I to choose among all the damsels and ladies of the world, thee would I choose," cried Powell.

After that, it was agreed that, when a year had sped, Powell should go to the Palace of the August and Venerable One of old, and claim her for his bride.

So, when twelve months had passed, Powell with his retinue of a hundred knights, all splendidly horsed and finely appareled, presented himself before the castle. There he found his fair lady and a feast already prepared at which he sat with her. On the other side of the table, were her father and mother.

In the midst of this joyous occasion, when all was gayety, and they talked together, in strode a youth clad in sheeny satin. He was of noble bearing and had auburn hair. He saluted Powell and his knights courteously.

At once Powell, the lord of Narberth, invited the stranger to come and sit down as guest beside him.

"Not so," replied the youth. "I am a suitor, and have come to crave a boon of thee."

Without guile or suspicion, Powell replied innocently.

"Ask what you will. If in my power, it shall be yours."

But Rhiannon chided Powell. She asked, "Oh, why did you give him such an answer?"

"But he did give it," cried the auburn haired youth. Then turning to the whole company of nobles, he appealed to them:

"Did he not pledge his word, before you all, to give me what I asked?"

Then, turning to Powell, he said:

"The boon I ask is this, to have thy bride, Rhiannon. Further, I want this feast and banquet to celebrate, in this place, our wedding."

At this demand, Powell seemed to have been struck dumb. He did not speak, but Rhiannon did.

"Be silent, as long as thou wilt," she cried, "but surely no man ever made worse use of his wits than thou hast done; for this man, to whom thou gavest thy oath of promise, is none other than Gwawl, the son of Clud. He is the suitor, from whom I fled to come to you, while you sat on the Narberth mound."

Now, out of such trouble, how should the maiden, promised to two men, be delivered?

Her wit saved her for the nonce. Powell was bound to keep his word; but Rhiannon explained to Gwawl, that it was not his castle or hall. So, he could not give the banquet; but, in a year from that date, if Gwawl would come for her, she would be his bride. Then, a new bridal feast would be set for the wedding.

In the meantime, Rhiannon planned with Powell to get out of the trouble. For this purpose, she gave him a magical bag, which he was to use when the right time should come.

Quickly the twelve months passed and then Gwawl appeared again, to claim his bride, and a great feast was spread in his honor.

All were having a good time, when in the midst of their merriment, a beggar appeared in the hall. He was in rags, and carried the usual beggar's wallet for food or alms. He asked only that, out of the abundance on the table, his bag might be filled.

Gwawl agreed, and ordered his servants to attend to the matter.

But the bag never got full. What they put into it, or how much made no difference. Dish after dish was emptied. By degrees, most of the food on the table was in the beggar's bag.

"My soul alive! Will that bag never get full?" asked Gwawl.

"No, by Heaven! Not unless some rich man shall get into it,

stamp it down with his feet, and call out 'enough.'"

Then Rhiannon, who sat beside Gwawl, urged him to attempt the task, by putting his two feet in the bag to stamp it down.

No sooner had Gwawl done this, than the supposed beggar pushed him down inside the bag. Then drawing the mouth shut, he tied it tight over Gwawl's head.

Then the beggar's rags dropped, and there stood forth the handsome leader, Powell. He blew his horn, and in rushed his knights who overcame and bound the followers of Gwawl.

Then they proceeded to play a merry game of football, using the bag, in which Gwawl was tied, as men in our day kick pigskin. One called to his mate, or rival, "What's in the bag?" and others answered, "a badger." So they played the game of "Badger in the Bag," kicking it around the hall.

They did not let the prisoner out of the bag, until he had promised to pay the pipers, the harpers, and the singers, who should come to the wedding of Powell and Rhiannon. He must give up all his claims, and register a vow never to take revenge. This oath given, and promises made, the bag was opened and the agreements solemnly confirmed in presence of all.

Then Gwawl, and every one of his men, knights and servants, were let go, and they went back to their own country.

A few evenings later, in the large banqueting hall, Powell and Rhiannon were married. Besides the great feast, presents were given to all present, high and low. Then the happy pair made their wedding journey to Gwawl's palace at Narberth. There the lovely bride gave a ring, or a gem, to every lord and lady in her new realm, and everybody was happy.

WHY THE BACK DOOR WAS FRONT

In the days when there were no books, or writing, and folk tales were the only ones told, there was an old woman, who had a bad reputation. She pretended to be very poor, so as not to attract or tempt robbers. Yet those who knew her best, knew also, as a subject of common talk, that she was always counting out her coins.

Besides this, she lived in a nice house, and it was believed that she made a living by stealing babies out of their cradles to sell to the bad fairies.

It was matter of rumor that she would, for an extra large sum, take a wicked fairy's ugly brat, and put it in place of a mother's darling.

In addition to these horrid charges against her, it was rumored that she laid a spell, or charm, on the cattle of people whom she did not like, in order to take revenge on them.

The old woman denied all this, and declared it was only silly gossip of envious people who wanted her money. She lived so comfortably, she averred, because her son, who was a stone mason, who made much money by building chimneys, which had then first come into fashion. When he brought to her the profits of his jobs, she counted the coins, and because of this, some people were jealous, and told bad stories about her. She declared she was thrifty, but neither a miser, nor a kidnaper, nor a witch.

One day, this old woman wanted more feathers to stuff into

her bed, to make it softer and feel pleasanter for her old bones to rest upon, for what she slept on was nearly worn through. So she went to a farm, where they were plucking geese, and asked for a few handfuls of feathers.

But the rich farmer's people refused and ordered her out of the farm yard.

Shortly after this event, the cows of this farmer, who was opposed to chimneys, and did not like her or her son, suffered dreadfully from the disease called the black quarter. As they had no horse doctors or professors of animal economy, or veterinaries in those days, many of the cows died. The rich farmer lost much money, for he had now no milk or beef to sell. At once, he suspected that his cattle were bewitched, and that the old woman had cast a spell on them. In those days, it was very easy to think so.

So the angry man went one day to the old crone, when she was alone, and her stout son was away on a distant job. He told her to remove the charm, which she had laid on his beasts, or he would tie her arms and legs together, and pitch her into the river.

The old woman denied vehemently that she possessed any such powers, or had ever practiced such black arts.

To make sure of it, the farmer made her say out loud, "The Blessing of God be upon your cattle!" To clinch the matter, he compelled her to repeat the Lord's Prayer, which she was able to do, without missing one syllable. She used the form of words which are not found in the prayer book, but are in the Bible, and was very earnest, when she prayed "Forgive us our debts, as we forgive our debtors."

But after all that trouble, and the rough way which the rich farmer took to save his cattle, his efforts were in vain. In spite of that kind of religion which he professed—which was shown by bullying a poor old woman—his cattle were still sick, with no sign of improvement. He was at his wits' end to know what to do next.

Now, as we have said, this was about the time that chimneys came into fashion. In very old days, the Cymric house was a round hut, with a thatched roof, without glass windows, and the smoke got out through the door and holes in the walls, in the best way it could. The only tapestry in the hut was in the shape of long festoons of soot, that hung from the roof or rafters. These, when the wind blew, or the fire was lively, would swing or dance or whirl, and often fall on the heads, or into the food, while the folks were eating. When the children cried, or made wry faces at the black stuff, their daddy only laughed, and said it was healthy, or was for good luck.

But by and by, the carpenters and masons made much improvement, especially when, instead of flint hatchets, they had iron axes and tools. Then they hewed down trees, that had thick cross branches and set up columns in the center, and made timber walls and rafters. Then the house was square or oblong. In other words, the Cymric folks squared the circle.

Now they began to have lattices, and, much later, even glass windows. They removed the fireplace from the middle of the floor and set it at the end of the house, opposite the door, and built chimneys.

Then they set the beds at the side, and made sleeping rooms. This was done by stretching curtains between partitions. They had also a loft, in which to keep odds and ends. They hung up the bacon and hams, and strings of onions, and made a mantle piece over the fireplace. They even began to decorate the walls with pictures and to set pewter dishes, china cats, and Dresden shepherds in rows on the shelves for ornaments.

Now people wore shoes and the floor, instead of being muddy, or dusty, with pools and puddles of water in the time of rainy weather and with the pigs and chickens running in and out, was of clay, beaten down flat and hard, and neatly white-washed at the edges. Outside, in front, were laid nice flat flag-stones, that made a pleasant path to the front door. Flowers, inside and out, added to the beauty of the home and made perfume for those who loved them.

The rich farmer had just left his old round hut and now lived in one of the new and better kind of houses. He was very proud of his chimney, which he had built higher than any of his neighbors, but he could not be happy, while so many of his cows were sick or dying. Besides, he was envious of other people's prosperity and cared nothing, when they, too, suffered.

One night, while he was standing in front of his fine house and wondering why he must be vexed with so many troubles, he talked to himself and, speaking out loud, said:

"Why don't my cows get well?"

"I'll tell you," said a voice behind him. It seemed half way between a squeak and a growl.

He turned round and there he saw a little, angry man. He was dressed in red, and stood hardly as high as the farmer's knee. The little old man glared at the big fellow and cried out in a high tone of voice:

"You must change your habits of disposing of your garbage, for other people have chimneys besides you."

"What has that to do with sickness among my cows?"

"Much indeed. Your family is the cause of your troubles, for they throw all their slops down my chimney and put out my fire."

The farmer was puzzled beyond the telling, for he owned all the land within a mile, and knew of no house in sight.

"Put your foot on mine, and then you will have the power of vision, to see clearly."

The farmer's big boot was at once placed on the little man's slipper, and when he looked down he almost laughed at the con-trast in size. What was his real surprise, when he saw that the slops thrown out of his house, did actually fall down; and, be-sides, the contents of the full bucket, when emptied, kept on dripping into the chimney of a house which stood far below, but which he had never seen before.

But as soon as he took his foot off that of the tiny little man, he saw nothing. Everything like a building vanished as in a dream.

"I see that my family have done wrong and injured yours. Pray forgive me. I'll do what I can to make amends for it."

"It's no matter now, if you only do as I ask you. Shut up your front door, build a wall in its place, and then my family will not suffer from yours."

The rich farmer thought all this was very funny, and he had a hearty laugh over it all.

Yet he did exactly as the little man in the red cloak had so politely asked him. He walled up the old door at the front, and built another at the back of the house, which opened out into the garden. Then he made the path, on which to go in from the roadway to the threshold, around the corners and over a longer line of flagstones. Then he removed the fireplace and chimney to what had been the front side of the house, but was now the back. For the next thing, he had a copper doorsill nailed down, which his housemaid polished, until it shone as bright as gold.

Yet long before this, his cows had got well, and they now gave more and richer milk than ever. He became the wealthiest man in the district. His children all grew up to be fine looking men and women. His grandsons were famous engineers and introduced paving and drainage in the towns so that to-day, for both man and beast, Wales is one of the healthiest of countries.

22

THE RED BANDITS OF
MONTGOMERY

When chimneys were first added to houses in Wales, and the style of house-building changed, from round to square, many old people found fault with the new fashion of letting the smoke out.

They declared they caught colds and sneezed oftener, than in the times gone by. The chimneys, they said, cost too much money, and were useless extravagances. They got along well enough, in the good old days, when the smoke had its own way of getting out. Then, it took plenty of time to pass through the doors and windholes, for no one person or thing was in a hurry, when they were young. Moreover, when the fireplace was in the middle of the floor, the whole family sat around it and had a so-ciable time.

It was true, as they confessed, when argued with, that the smell of the cooking used to linger too long. The soot also, hung in long streamers from the rafters, and stuck to the house, like old friends.

But the greatest and most practical objection of the old folks to the chimneys was that robbers used them to climb down at night and steal people's money, when they were asleep. So, many householders used to set old scythe blades across the new smoke holes, to keep out the thieves, or to slice them up, if they persisted.

In Montgomery, which is one of the Welsh shires, there was an epidemic of robbery, and the doings of the Red Bandits are famous in history.

Now there was a young widow, whose husband had been killed by the footpads, or road robbers. She was left alone in the world, with a little boy baby in the cradle and only one cow in the byre. She had hard work to pay her rent, but as there were three or four scythes set in the chimney, and the cow stable had a good lock on it, she thought she was safe from burglars or common thieves.

But the Reds picked out the most expert chimney-climber in their gang, and he one night slipped down into the widow's cottage, without making any noise or cutting off his nose, toes, or fingers. Then, robbing the widow of her rent money, he picked the lock of the byre and drove off the cow. In the morning, the poor woman found both doors open, but there was no money and no cow.

While she was crying over her loss, and wringing her hands, because of her poverty, she heard a knock at the door.

"Come in," said the widow.

There entered an old lady with a kindly face. She was very tall and well dressed. Her cloak, her gloves, and shoes, and the ruffles under her high peaked Welsh head dress, were all green. The widow thought she looked like an animated leek. In her right hand was a long staff, and in her left, under her cloak, she held a little bag, that was green, also.

"Why do you weep?" asked the visitor.

Then the widow told her tale of woe—the story of the loss of her husband, and how a red robber, in spite of the scythe blades set in the chimney, had come down and taken away both her money and her cow.

Now, although she had sold all her butter and cream, she could neither pay her rent, nor have any buttermilk with her rye bread and flummery.

"Dry your tears and take comfort," said the tall lady in the green peaked hat. "Here is money enough to pay your rent and buy another cow." With that, she sat down at the round table near the peat fire. Opening her bag, the shining gold coins slid out and formed a little heap on the table.

"There, you can have all this, if you will give me all I want."

At first, the widow's eyes opened wide, and then she glanced at the cradle, where her baby was sleeping. Then she wondered, though she said nothing.

But the next moment, she was laughing at herself, and looking around at her poor cottage. She tried to guess what there was in it, that the old lady could possibly want.

"You can have anything I have. Name it," she said cheerfully to her visitor.

But only a moment more, and all her fears returned at the thought that the visitor might ask for her boy.

The old lady spoke again and said:

"I want to help you all I can, but what I came here for is to get the little boy in the cradle."

The widow now saw that the old woman was a fairy, and that if her visitor got hold of her son, she would never see her child again.

So she begged piteously of the old lady, to take anything and everything, except her one child.

"No, I want that boy, and, if you want the gold, you must let me take him."

"Is there anything else that I can do for you, so that I may get the money?" asked the widow.

"Well, I'll make it easier for you. There are two things I must tell you to cheer you."

"What are they?" asked the widow, eagerly.

"One is, that by our fairy law, I cannot take your boy, until three days have passed. Then, I shall come again, and you shall have the gold; but only on the one condition I have stated."

"And the next?" almost gasped the widow.

"If you can guess my name, you will doubly win; for then, I

shall give you the gold and you can keep your boy."

Without waiting for another word, the lady in green scooped up her money, put it back in the bag, and moved off and out the door.

The poor woman, at once a widow and mother, and now stripped of her property, fearing to lose her boy, brooded all night over her troubles and never slept a wink.

In the morning, she rose up, left her baby with a neighbor, and went to visit some relatives in the next village, which was several miles distant. She told her story, but her kinsfolk were too poor to help her. So, all disconsolate, she turned her face homewards.

On her way back she had to pass through the woods, where, on one side, was a clearing. In the middle of this open space, was a ring of grass. In the ring a little fairy lady was tripping around and singing to herself.

Creeping up silently, the anxious mother heard to her joy, a rhymed couplet and caught the sound of a name, several times repeated. It sounded like "Silly Doot."

Hurrying home and perfectly sure that she knew the secret that would save her boy, she set cheerily about her regular work and daily tasks. In fact, she slept soundly that night.

Next day, in came the lady in green as before, with her bag of money. Taking her seat at the round table, near the fire, she poured out the gold. Then jingling the coins in the pile, she said:

"Now give up your boy, or guess my name, if you want me to help you."

The young widow, feeling sure that she had the old fairy in a trap, thought she would have some fun first.

"How many guesses am I allowed?" she asked.

"All you want, and as many as you please," answered the green lady, smiling.

The widow rattled off a string of names, English, Welsh and Biblical; but every time the fairy shook her head. Her eyes began to gleam, as if she felt certain of getting the boy. She even moved her chair around to the side nearest the cradle.

"One more guess," cried the widow. "Can it be Silly Doot?"

At this sound, the fairy turned red with rage. At the same moment, the door opened wide and a blast of wind made the hearth fire flare up. Leaving her gold behind her, the old woman flew up the chimney, and disappeared over the housetops.

The widow scooped up the gold, bought two cows, furnished her cottage with new chairs and fresh flowers, and put the rest of the coins away under one of the flag stones at the hearth. When her boy grew up, she gave him a good education, and he became one of the fearless judges, who, with the aid of Baron Owen, rooted out of their lair the Red Bandits, that had robbed his mother. Since that day, there has been little crime in Wales —the best governed part of the kingdom.

23

THE FAIRY CONGRESS

O ne can hardly think of Wales without a harp. The music of this most ancient and honorable instrument, which emits sweet sounds, when heard in a foreign land makes Welsh folks homesick for the old country and the music of the harp. Its strings can wail with woe, ripple with merriment, sound out the notes of war and peace, and lift the soul in heavenly melody.

Usually a player on the harp opened the Eistedfodd, as the Welsh literary congress is called, but this time they had engaged for the fairies a funny little fellow to start the programme with a solo on his violin.

The figure of this musician, at the congress of Welsh fairies, was the most comical of any in the company. The saying that he was popular with all the mountain spirits was shown to be true, the moment he began to scrape his fiddle, for then they all crowded around him.

"Did you ever see such a tiny specimen?" asked Queen Mab of Puck.

The little fiddler came forward and drawing his instrument from under his arm, proceeded to scrape the strings. He had on a pair of moss trousers, and his coat was a yellow gorse flower. His feet were clad in shoes made of beetles' wings, which always kept bright, as if polished with a brush.

When one looked at the fiddle, he could see that it was only a wooden spoon, with strings across the bowl. But the moment he drew the bow from one side to the other, all the elves, from every part of the hills, came tripping along to hear the music, and at once began dancing.

Some of these elves were dressed in pink, some in blue, others in yellow, and many had glow worms in their hands. Their tread was so light that the flower stems never bent, nor was a petal crushed, when they walked over the turf. All, as they came near, bowed or dropped a curtsey. Then the little musician took off his cap to each, and bowed in return.

There was too much business before the meeting for dancing to be kept up very long, but when the violin solo was over, at a sign given by the fiddler, the dancers took seats wherever they could find them, on the grass, or gorse, or heather, or on the stones. After order had been secured, the chairman of the meeting read regrets from those who had been invited but could not be present.

The first note was from the mermaids, who lived near the Green Isles of the Ocean. They asked to be excused from traveling inland and climbing rocks. In the present delicate state of their health this would be too fatiguing. Poor things!

It was unanimously voted that they be excused.

Queen Mab was dressed, as befitted the occasion, like a Welsh lady, not wearing a crown, but a high peaked hat, pointed at the top and about half a yard high. It was black and was held on by fastenings of scalloped lace, that came down around her neck.

The lake fairies, or Elfin Maids, were out in full force. These lived at the bottom of the many ponds and pools in Wales. Many stories are told of the wonderful things they did with boats and cattle.

Nowadays, when they milk cows by electric machinery and use steam launches on the water, most of the water sprites of all kinds have been driven away, for they do not like the smell of kerosene or gasoline. It is for these reasons that, in our day, they are not often seen. In fact, cows from the creameries can wade out into the water and even stand in it, while lashing their tails to keep off the flies, without any danger, as in old times, of being pulled down by the Elfin Maids.

The little Red Men, that could hide under a thimble, and have plenty of room to spare, were all out. The elves, and nixies and sprites, of all colors and many forms were on hand.

The pigmies, who guard the palace of the king of the world underground, came in their gay dresses. There were three of them, and they brought in their hands balls of gold, with which to play tenpins, but they were not allowed to have any games while the meeting was going on.

In fact, just when these little fellows from down under the earth were showing off their gay clothes and their treasures from the caves, one mischievous fairy maid sidled up to their chief and whispered in his ear:

"Better put away your gold, for this is in modern Wales, where they have pawn shops. Three golden balls, two above the one below, which you often see nowadays, mean that two to one you will never get it again. These hang out as the sign of a pawnbroker's shop, and what you put in does not, as a rule, come out. I am afraid that some of the Cymric fairies from Cornwall, or Montgomery, or Cheshire, might think you were after business, and you understand that no advertising is allowed here."

In a moment, each of the three leaders thrust his ball into his bosom. It made his coat bulge out, and at this, some of the fairies wondered, but all they thought of was that this spoiled a handsome fellow's figure. Or was it some new idea? To tell the truth, they were vexed at not keeping up with the new fashions, for they knew nothing of this latest fad among such fine young gallants.

Much of the chat and gossip, before and after the meeting, was between the fairies who live in the air, or on mountains, and those down in the earth, or deep in the sea. They swapped news, gossip and scandal at a great rate.

There were a dozen or two fine-looking creatures who had high brows, who said they were Co-eds. This did not mean that these fairies had ever been through college. "Certainly the college never went through them," said one very homely fairy, who was spiteful and jealous. The simple fact was that the one they called Betty, the Co-ed, and others from that Welsh village, called Bryn Mawr, and another from Flint, and another from Yale, and still others from Brimbo and from Co-ed Poeth, had come from places so named and down on the map of Wales, though they were no real Co-ed girls there, that could talk French, or English, or read Latin. In fact, Co-ed simply meant that they were from the woods and lived among the trees; for Co-ed in Welsh means a forest.

The fairy police were further instructed not to admit, and, if such were found, to put out the following bad characters, for this was a perfectly respectable meeting. These naughty folks were:

The Old Hag of the Mist.

The Invisible Hag that moans dolefully in the night.

The Tolaeth, a creature never seen, but that groans, sings, saws, or stamps noisily.

The Dogs of the Sky.

All witches, of every sort and kind.

All peddlers of horseshoes, crosses, charms, or amulets.

All mortals with brains fuddled by liquor.

All who had on shoes which water would not run under.

All fairies that were accustomed to turn mortals into cheese.

Every one of these, who might want to get in, were to be refused admittance.

Another circle of rather exclusive fairies, who always kept away from the blacksmiths, hardware stores, smelting furnaces and mines, had formed an anti-iron society. These were a kind of a Welsh "Four Hundred," or élite, who would have nothing to do with anyone who had an iron tool, or weapon, or ornament in his hand, or on his dress, or who used iron in any form, or for any use. They frowned upon the idea of Cymric Land becoming rich by mining, and smelting, and selling iron. They did not even approve of the idea that any imps and dwarfs of the iron mines should be admitted to the meeting.

One clique of fairies, that looked like elves were in bad humor, almost to moping. When one of these got up to speak, it seemed as if he would never sit down. He tired all the lively fairies by long-winded reminiscences, of druids, and mistletoes, and by telling every one how much better the old times were than the present.

President Puck, who always liked things short, and was himself as lively as quicksilver, many times called these long-winded fellows to order; but they kept meandering on, until daybreak, when it was time to adjourn, lest the sunshine should spoil them all, and change them into slate or stone.

It was hard to tell just how much business was disposed of, at this session, or whether one ever came to the point, although there was a great deal of oratory and music. Much of what was said was in poetry, or in verses, or rhymes, of three lines each. What they talked about was mainly in protest against the smoke of factories and collieries, and because there was so much soot, and so little soap, in the land.

But what did they do at the fairy congress?

The truth is, that nobody to-day knows what was done in this session of the fairies, for the proceedings were kept secret. The only one who knows was an old Welshman whom the story-teller used to meet once in a while. He is the one mortal who knows anything about this meeting, and he won't tell; or at least he won't talk in anything but Welsh. So we have to find out the gist of the matter, by noticing, in the stories which we have just read what the fairies did.

THE SWORD OF AVALON

Many of the Welsh tales are about fighting and wars and no country as small as Wales has so many castles. Yet these are nearly all in ruins and children play in them. This is because men got tired of battles and sieges.

Everybody knows that after King Arthur's knights had punched and speared, whacked and chopped at each other with axe and sword long enough, had slain dragons and tamed mon - sters, and rescued princesses from cruel uncles, and good men from dark dungeons, even the plain people, such as farmers and mechanics, had enough and wanted no more. Besides this, they wished to be treated more like human beings, and not have to work so hard and also to keep their money when they earned it.

Even King Arthur himself, towards the end of this era, saw that fashions were changing and that he must change with them. Hardware was too high in price, and was no longer needed for clothing. He was wise enough to see that battle axes, maces, swords, lances and armor had better be put to some bet - ter use, when iron was getting scarce and wool and linen were cheaper. Even the stupid Normans learned that decency and kindness cost less, and accomplished more in making the Welshery loyal subjects of the king.

So when, after many battles, King Arthur went out to have a little war of his own, and to enjoy the fight, in which he was mortally wounded, he showed his greatness, even in the hour of death. In truth, it is given to some men, like Samson, to be even mightier when they die, than when following the strenuous life. So it was with this great and good man of Cymry. His love for his people never ceased for one moment, and in his dying hour he left a bequest that all his people have understood and acted upon.

Thus it has come to pass that the Welsh have been really unconquerable, by Saxon or Norman, or even in these twentieth century days by Teutons. Though living in a small country, they are among the greatest in the world, not in force, or in material things, but in soul. When Belgium was invaded, they not only stood up in battle against the invader, but they welcomed to their homes tens of thousands of fugitives and fed and sheltered them.

Brave as lions, their path of progress has been in faithfulness to duty, industry, and patience, and along the paths of poetry, music and brotherhood. Their motto for ages has been, "Truth against the World."

Now the manner of King Arthur's taking off and his immortal legacy was on this fashion:

After doing a great many wonderful things, in many countries, King Arthur came back to punish the wicked man, Modred. In the battle that ensued, he received wounds that made him feel that he was very soon to die. So he ordered his loyal vassal to take his sword to the island of Avalon. There he must cast the weapon into the deep water.

But the sword was part of the soul of Arthur. It would not sink out of sight, until it had given a message, from their king to the Welsh, for all time.

After it had been thrown in the water, it disappeared, but rose again. First the shining blade, and then the hilt, and then a hand was seen to rise out of the flood.

Thrice that hand waved the sword round and round.

This was the prophecy of "the deathless from the dead." King Arthur's body might be hid in a cave, or molder in the ground, but his soul was to live and cheer his people. His beloved Cymric nation, with their undying language, were to rise in power again.

And the resurrection has been glorious. Not by the might of the soldier, or by arms or war—though the Welsh never flinch from duty, or before the foe—but by the power of poet, singer and the narrator of stories, that touch the imagination, and fire the soul to noble deeds, have these results come.

Arthur's good blade, thus waved above the waters, became a veritable sword of the Spirit.

Men of genius arose to flush with color the old legends. Prophets, preachers, monks, missionaries carried these all over Europe, and made them the vehicles of Christian doctrine. In their new forms, they fired the imagination and illuminated, as with ten thousand lamps, many lands and nations, until they held every people in spell. In miracle and morality play, they re-appeared in beauty. They attuned the harp and instrument of the musician and the troubadour, and these sang the gospel in all lands, north and south, while telling the stories of Adam, and of Abraham, of Bethlehem, and of the cross, of the Holy Grail, and of Arthur and his Knights. All the precious lore of the Celtic race became transfigured, to illustrate and enforce Christian truth. The symbolical bowl, the Celtic caldron of abundance, became the cup of the Eucharist and the Grail the symbol of blessings eternal.

By the artists, in the stained glass, and in windows of the great churches, which were built no longer of wood but of stone, that blossomed under the chisel, the old legends were, by the new currents of truth, given a mystic glow. As wonderful as the rise of Gothic architecture and the upbuilding of cathedrals, as glorious as the light and art, that beautify the great temples of worship, was this re-birth of the Arthurian legends.

For now, again, the old virtues of the knightly days—loyalty, obedience, redress of wrongs, reverence of womanhood, and the application of Christian ethics to the old rude rules of decency, lifted the life of the common people to a nobler plane and ushered in the modern days.

Then, after seven hundred years, a host of singers, Tennyson leading them all, attuned the old Celtic harp. They reset for us the Cymric melody and colorful incidents in "the light that never was on sea or land." The old days live again in a greater glory.

Lady Guest put the Mabinogion into English, and Renan, and Arnold, and Rolleston, and Rhys, in prose, competed in praise of the heritages from the old time. Popular education was diffused. The Welsh language rose again from the dead. Cardiff holds in pure white marble the most thrilling interpretation of Welsh history, in the twelve white marble statues of the great men of Wales. The Welsh people, by bloodless victory, have won the respect of all mankind.

They set a beacon for the oppressed nations. In the World War of 1914-1918, they helped to save freedom and civilization. They were in the van.

Long may the sword of Arthur wave!

Printed in Great Britain
by Amazon